Dave Stevens' The Rocketeer®

ART & STORY BY STEPHEN MOONEY

@IDWpublishing
IDWpublishing.com

978-1-68405-944-7 26 25 24 23 1 2 3 4

For international rights, contact licensing@idwpublishing.com.

Special thanks to Jennifer Bawcum, David Mandel, and Kelvin Mao.

THE ROCKETEER: THE GREAT RACE TPB. JANUARY 2023. FIRST PRINTING.

LETTERING & DESIGN BY
SHAWN LEE

EDITORIAL ASSISTANT
NICOLAS NIÑO

EDITOR
SCOTT DUNBIER

COLORS BY LEN O'GRADY

For our newest
little Rocketeer--
James Brendan Mooney,
born during the
production of this book.
--Stephen Mooney

THE ROCKETEER
THE GREAT RACE COLLECTED EDITION

Introduction
by Stephen Mooney

So, that Dave Stevens guy could really *draw,* huh?

I've been a massive *Rocketeer* fan since I first started collecting American comics in earnest in the early 1990s. I never actually encountered the original issues in the wild, so it was the early collected editions that first brought Cliff and his pals to my attention.

Boy, oh boy, those books blew me away. I'd been in love with the 1930s American industrial design aesthetic from a very early age, and to see it so beautifully form the basis for Dave's world was incredibly exciting and romantic. The cars, the planes—the women! All expertly rendered through Dave's beautiful line. This stuff was next level.

I've always been primarily an artwork fan when it comes to comic books, and to this day, I still recognize Dave Stevens as one of the very best practitioners of our craft. He could draw the absolute hell outta *anything,* always imbuing even the most mundane item or setting with that slick, glossy magic of his. I yearned to be anything *approaching* that good.

I got older and started my own book set in that same period of American history, *Half Past Danger.* A ton of different books and movies influenced my own project, but perhaps none more so than *The Rocketeer*—the scrappy, reluctant (oblivious?) hero that lands the gig almost by default and simply wants to find the quickest and least deadly way out. Saving the world is merely a means to an end, a byproduct of saving his own ass.

Cliff Secord as the Rocketeer is a shining, perfect example of that archetype, and I loved him from day one. He's the kind of guy you'd doubtfully, reluctantly accept as a partner but wind up beyond grateful that you did.

Then there's one of the very best supporting casts in comics: the gruff, oughta-know-better father figure of Peevy, the oddball collection of down-and-outs and stalwarts that form the flying circus, that goddamn rat Marco, and the government stooges that hound Cliff every step of the way.

And then there's Betty. Even as a kid, I knew there was something a little bit different about this lady. A little bit *special.* The twinkle in the eye. The promise in the smile and the figure in the dress. Equal parts playful and dangerous. In other words, *perfect.*

So cut to 2021, and I'm chatting on the socials with my friend and fellow Irish comic book apologist Declan Shalvey. We somehow arrived on the subject of *The Rocketeer,* and Dec casually observed that I'd be a perfect fit for that book. Why had I never done one?

I scoffed, of course, at his utter naivete. "You don't just 'decide' to work on one of your dream books, Declan. Those projects are destined to remain out of reach for mortals such as us." Pie in the proverbial sky. Another member of our chat, Chase Marotz, who happens to be an editor at IDW, who has the *Rocketeer* license, piped up, "Actually… I've heard worse ideas."

So Chase and I floated a couple of ideas to Scott Dunbier, Special Projects Editor, Grand Poohbah and arbiter of all things Rocketeer at IDW.

He liked what he heard and saw, and it was that simple. We were off to the Great Races.

So, I had the gig. Crap… I had the gig! What the hell was I supposed to do with it?! Sure, I had a decent and solid premise… but now I had to actually *make* the bloody thing!

The absolute pressure. All lumped on myself by myself, but pressure, nonetheless. Firstly, and above all, the pressure to do Dave and his estate proud: I'd been entrusted with these beloved characters, and by all that's holy, I wasn't gonna be the sap to mess it up.

Secondly, though, the pressure to live up to that incredible legacy. I was confident enough that I could tell a decent story, but there was just no way I'd ever be able to compare to Dave artistically (though in my defense, who could?). I'd have to put absolutely everything I had into these pages.

Dave Stevens was notoriously slow. And listen, that kind of relentless perfectionism takes time. *Lots* of time. In modern comics, you do not have lots of time. In my grand scheme, my *Rocketeer* story was to be (as I envisioned it, anyway) the third big chapter in Cliff and Betty's lives, after the original story and *Cliff's New York Adventure.* I wanted to pick up pretty much right after that point and show where the gang goes from there.

So yeah, pressure.

The first issue of *Rocketeer* took me nine weeks to draw, the longest I've ever spent on 22 pages in my life. Dave probably had a year to do that much… Still, it was the best I could do, and I remain at least somewhat satisfied with it. I spent between six to eight weeks on each of the remaining three issues.

It was a goddamn blast. I enjoyed it almost as much as working on my own book, and that never really happens. You take a work-for-hire gig from Marvel or DC or whoever, and you give it absolutely everything you've got, but it never really feels like your own baby. *Rocketeer* felt different for some reason, like I was really able to bring my own sensibilities and quirks to it. It was still most definitely Dave's book, but it was *my* version of Dave's book.

Working with some of the very best pros in comics certainly didn't hurt. I've wanted to work on a project with Scott Dunbier since I was about 15, when he was the editor of the WildStorm and Cliffhanger lines of books. America's Best Comics, indeed. As well as being one of the best editors in the business, Scott is unquestionably one of the finest raconteurs. Our calls about the book would inevitably finish with a few of his mind-blowing tales of the greats of comics past and present. Just great, great stuff.

Len O'Grady, yet another Irishman and one hell of a colorist, and book designer/letterer extraordinaire Shawn Lee rounded out our creative team, and I couldn't be more pleased with the results. Len brought something indefinably brilliant to each and every page, instantly improving and embellishing all that I had drawn. Shawn turned the entire enterprise into a beautiful and inviting package, warm with the nostalgia and design ethos of an imagined time long past.

It meant an awful lot to me, working on this book. I loved every minute of it. It isn't often that you get to tick one of those almighty bucket-listers off, but I couldn't appreciate the opportunity more.

Dave Stevens remains a mighty totem in my life, one that casts a long, heavy shadow. He's also one of the most inspiring people I never met.

I hope I did him proud.

Stephen Mooney
Dublin, June 2022

ART BY GABRIEL RODRÍGUEZ COLORS BY LEN O'GRADY

...AND WHAT OF THESE SEEMINGLY FANTASTIC REPORTS OF HONEST-TO-GOODNESS FOREIGN SPIES, RIGHT HERE IN CALIFORNIA?
WARTIME PARANOIA?
POLITICAL SCAREMONGERING, AS THE GOVERNOR HAS BRANDED IT?
BIGELOW

RUSTIC CANYON, LOS ANGELES, IS THE ALLEGED LOCATION OF THIS EGREGIOUS ASSAULT ON NATIONAL AND MORAL VALUES.
EYE WITNESSES CLAIM TO HAVE SEEN GLIMPSES OF PURPORTED UNIFORMED SOLDIERS ON MANEUVERS IN THE HILLS.
GERMAN SCOUTING OPERATIONS PERHAPS, NIBBLING AT POTENTIAL ENEMY LINES?

THE UNMITIGATED GALL AND SHEER CHUTZPAH REQUIRED TO ESTABLISH SUCH BOOTS ON THE GROUND IN U.S. TERRITORY, IS, IN THIS REPORTER'S OPINION, A WORK OF PURE FICTION.
BUT IT DOES FURTHER ILLUSTRATE THE LOOMING SPECTRE OF THE WAR IN EUROPE AND OUR POTENTIAL EXPOSURE TO IT.

WHILE IT WOULD BE A SATIRIC TURN OF FATE'S WHEEL INDEED, WERE IT PROVED THAT THESE RUMORS HELD ANY MERIT--
--IT SEEMS FAIR TO SURMISE THAT, FOR NOW, AT LEAST--
--THE BOOGEYMAN REMAINS AT ARM'S LENGTH.

ROOAARR
CLIFF, YA LUNATIC!
THIS AIN'T YER PROBLEM--LEAVE IT TO THE FEDS!

AAAHH, CLIFF!
THAT BOY'S FINALLY GONNA GO AN' GET HIMSELF KILLED.
FWOOOSH

THE ROCKETEER SOARS.

THIS IS WHERE THOSE KIDS SAID THEY SAW THE KRAUTS--
--BUT IT ALL LOOKS PRETTY QUIET DOWN THERE.
IT'S LIKELY A BUNCH'A SOAP--
--BUT I'M NOT TAKIN' ANY CHANCES AFTER THE LOCUST HUBBUB.
IF THESE GOOSE-STEPPERS REALLY DO HAVE THE NERVE TA SET UP CAMP ON OUR FRONT YARD--
--THEY'LL HAVE
THE ROCKETEER
TO ANSWER TO!
YOUR OWN RISK
HEY--

HANDS--
--OFF!
‹HOLD HIM!›*
OOFF
*TRANSLATED FROM GERMAN.
HOLY SMOKES--
--YOU GUYS ARE THE REAL MCCO--
KLANG
--OOOY!
FWOOOSH
AAGH!
SORRY, FREUND--
--GOTTA FLY!
AARGH
OOFF
COMIN' THROUGH!
WHOOOSH
THIS PLACE REALLY IS A KNOCKOUT!
GOTT--
WHAM

I'D LOVE TO STAY AND POWWOW--
--BUT NOW THAT I'VE SEEN YOU HEINIES ARE FER REAL--
--TIME TO GET THE HECK OUTTA DODGE!
‹MOVE.›
UH-OH!
BRAKABRAKA
SO LONG, FELLAS!
IT'S BEEN A REAL--
PWANG
PWANG
PWANG
--PANIC!

THIS DOGGONED ROCKET HAS FINALLY DONE ME IN!
SURVIVED ORSINO'S DEATH TRAPS AN' YEARS OF TAKIN' MY LIFE IN MY HANDS AS A PROP-JOCKEY--
BIGELOW
--ONLY TO BE SHOT OUT OF THE SKY!
WHAT'LL OL' PEEV SAY--
--AN' BETTY!

WOTTA PRIZE CHUMP I AM--
--OFF PLAYING HERO WHEN I SHOULD'VE BEEN PLAYIN' HOMEMAKER.
NO WONDER SHE WANTED TA HEAD TA EUROPE WITH THAT RAT, MARCO...
IF I MAKE IT OUTTA THIS SCRAPE, I SWEAR I--
--AAAGHH!

--AAGH!
WHUMP
THEY SAY YER WHOLE LIFE FLASHES BEFORE YER EYES RIGHT BEFORE YA PUNCH YER TICKET AND I TELL YA--
--THEY AIN'T WRONG!
THAT'S IT, BETTY.
I'M ALL THE WAY DONE WITH THAT DAMNED ROCKET.
IT'S TIME I FOCUSED ON WHAT'S REALLY IMPORTANT-- YOU AN' ME.
SO WHAT MAKES THIS TIME ANY DIFFERENT?
YOU'VE MADE THESE PROMISES BEFORE, CLIFF, AND THEY'RE STARTING TO WEAR A LITTLE THIN.
WHY IS IT YOU JUST CAN'T RESIST PUTTING YOURSELF IN HARM'S WAY?
NAW, BETTS-- THIS TIME I MEAN IT!

OH, CLIFF-- IF THAT'S TRUE, THEN I'M GLAD.
TRULY.
BUT I CAN'T HELP THINKING ABOUT THAT CAMP YOU FOUND.
I CAN'T BELIEVE REAL NAZIS ARE OPERATING ON OUR OWN SOIL...!
IT SCARES ME, CLIFF.
WHO KNOWS HOW FAR THEIR INFLUENCE REACHES?
ME TOO, HONEY. BUT NOW THAT THE BRASS KNOW ABOUT THAT PLACE, THEY'LL FLUSH THOSE RATS OUT LICKETY-SPLIT.
WE DON'T NEED TO WORRY ABOUT THE REST A' THOSE LOONIES EVER SHOWIN' UP. THEY'D BE CRAZY TO TAKE US ON.
I HOPE YOU'RE RIGHT.
THE LAST THING I NEED FOR YOU TO DO IS ENLIST...!
HAW--FAT CHANCE A' THAT!
SOLDIERIN' IS A MUG'S GAME!

SO, YEH SCORED A BIG FAT LEMON WITH THAT ONE, HUH?
AH, PEEV--WHADDYA WANT?

COULDA SWORN YA WERE SPOSED TA TURN THIS BLAMED CONTRAPTION IN AT SOME POINT?
YA ONLY GONNA BE HAPPY ONCE IT KILLS YA?
I'VE DECIDED ENOUGH IS ENOUGH.

SURE, KID.
AIN'T NEVER HEARD THAT ONE BEFORE.
FOR REAL--THIS TIME I'M GONNA DO RIGHT BY BETTY AN' ME.

THE GREAT INTERNATIONAL AIR RACE
CALIFORNIA · NEW YORK · LONDON · PARIS
WINNER TAKES ALL
SO YOU'VE GOT ZERO INTEREST IN THIS, THEN.

LEMME SEE THAT!
WHOOEE!
BOY, COULD I USE--
THE GREAT INTERNATIONAL AIR RACE
CALIFORNIA · NEW YORK · LONDON · PARIS

--NO.
I PROMISED BETTY, SAVVY?
FROM HERE ON OUT, I'M TOEIN' THE LINE.
STRAIGHT AS AN ARROW.

--REPORTS COMING IN OF A FEDERAL RAID OPERATION ON A RANCH IN RUSTIC CANYON, WHERE--
HEY--TURN THAT UP, WOULDYA, PAL?
NNESS
MURPHY'S BAR, THAT EVENING.
--FOUND WHAT SOME ARE DESCRIBING AS ABANDONED NAZI MILITARY EQUIPMENT AND DOCU-MENTATION--
HUH.
SOUNDS LIKE THEY PACKED UP AN' BUGGED OUT.
AT LEAST SOME GOOD CAME FROM THE WHOLE SORRY EPISODE...
--WHILE FEDERAL AUTHORITIES HAVE YET TO COMMENT, THE GOVERNOR REITERATES HIS STANCE ON THE ENTIRE THING BEING A HOAX PERPETRATED BY LOCAL YAHOOS--
--SEEKING TO FUEL THE PERVADING SENSE OF PARANOIA OVER--KLIK
ONE A' THESE DAYS...
FEELS LIKE ONE A' THESE DAYS MY LUCK IS FINALLY GONNA GIVE OUT.
HUH?
GETTIN' JUMPY IN MY OLD AGE...
LVEY BROS
SO WHERE THE HECK DOES A SCHMO LIKE ME FIND HONEST WORK IN THIS TOWN...
...WORK THAT WON'T BORE ME TA TEARS!

NEXT MORNING.
CLIFF SECORD?
YOU IN HERE?
DEPENDS WHO'S ASKIN', PALLY.
I'M HERE AT THE BEHEST OF MY EMPLOYER, DELTON NKOSI.
WORLD-RENOWNED INDUSTRIALIST AND INVENTOR--
--I'M ASSUMING YOU'VE HEARD OF HIM?
SURE.
WHO HASN'T?
INDEED.
MR. NKOSI WOULD LIKE TO DISCUSS A POTENTIAL EMPLOYMENT OPPORTUNITY WITH YOU.
OH YEAH?
WHAT'S IT PAY?
WHY DON'T YOU ACCOMPANY ME TO HIS MANSION RIGHT NOW AND FIND OUT?

WHOO-EE-- THAT'S SOME SPREAD!
IS THAT BELLA ASSUAGE?
FINEST CANARY THIS TOWN HAS HEARD IN YEARS, ACCORDIN' TO OL' PEEV.
SURE AIN'T TOO HARD ON THE EYES, EITHER.
ENOUGH, DELTON!

I WON'T BE TREATED LIKE ONE OF YOUR SERVANTS!
THIS PLACE SURE IS SNAZZY...

MR. SECORD!
THANK YOU FOR ACCEPTING MY INVITATION!
PLEASURE TA MEET YA, MR. NKOSI.

SO WHAT'S THIS ALL ABOUT?
YOU WANT ME TA HELP TEST ONE A' YOUR INVENTIONS?
WHY, YES, AFTER A FASHION.
YOU'VE HEARD OF THE GREAT RACE?

YEAH, BUT I AIN'T--
HEAR ME OUT, MR. SECORD.
YOU STAND TO EARN A COOL $10,000, IF YOU HONOR MY REQUEST.

PHEEEE-OOOOO!
I THOUGHT THAT MIGHT GET YOUR ATTENTION.
YOU COME HIGHLY RECOMMENDED, MR. SECORD.
IF YOU'LL JUST STEP THIS WAY--
--I'D LIKE YOU TO REPRESENT ME IN THE RACE!
THE PRIZE IS AN ESSENTIAL COMPONENT IN A POTENTIALLY WORLD-CHANGING ENERGY TECHNOLOGY.
THE TROPHY AWARDED TO THE WINNER IS COMPRISED OF A PURE, EXCEPTIONALLY RARE ELEMENT.
THE LARGEST SINGLE SOURCE OF SAID ELEMENT AVAILABLE TO THE PUBLIC.
I NEED THIS ELEMENT TO COMPLETE MY LATEST AND GREATEST INVENTION!
THE RACE BEGINS IN CALIFORNIA, WITH A FUEL STOP IN NEW YORK, THEN ACROSS THE ATLANTIC TO ENGLAND--AND FINALLY ENDS IN PARIS, FRANCE.
THE JOURNEY OF A LIFETIME!
ONE OF A KIND!
IT'S A TEMPTIN' OFFER, BUT MY GEE BEE AIN'T BUILT FOR THAT KINDA RANGE.
!!!
IS THAT A BUGATTI MODEL 100?!
IN OUTWARD APPEARANCE YES, BUT ITS INNARDS ARE EXTENSIVELY MODIFIED ACCORDING TO MY OWN DESIGNS.
IF YOU ARE GOING TO WIN THE GREATEST AIR RACE IN THE HISTORY OF MANKIND, WHY NOT DO IT IN STYLE?

WHAT A BEAUTY!
HOLD ON--IS THAT A FUEL TANK RIGHT BEHIND THE COCKPIT?
ARE YOU INSANE?!
I'D BE SITTING ON A POWDER KEG AT 10,000 FEET!

MERELY ONE OF SEVERAL AUXILIARY TANKS.
THE FUEL REQUIREMENT FOR SUCH A LONG-DISTANCE FLIGHT IS EXTRA-ORDINARY.
I HAVE DEVELOPED A PROPRIETARY FUEL COMPOSITE THAT IS MIXED IN-FLIGHT WITH THE REGULAR FUEL--HENCE THE DIFFERENT COMPARTMENTS.
WITHOUT THIS UNIQUE AND QUITE BRILLIANT BLEND, THE NKOSI 5,000 CANNOT ACHIEVE ITS FULL, GLORIOUS POTENTIAL.

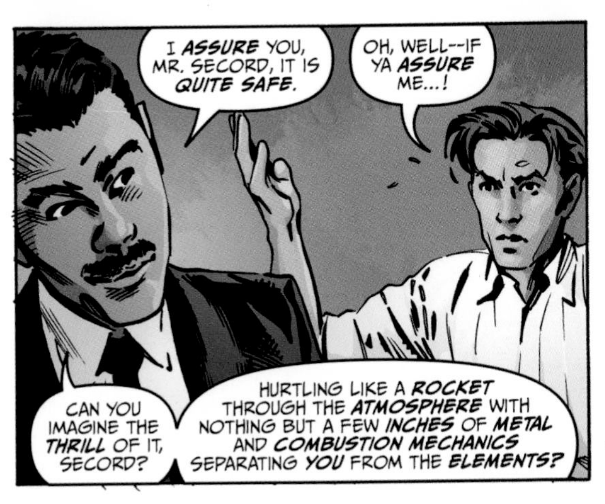
I ASSURE YOU, MR. SECORD, IT IS QUITE SAFE.
OH, WELL--IF YA ASSURE ME...!
CAN YOU IMAGINE THE THRILL OF IT, SECORD?
HURTLING LIKE A ROCKET THROUGH THE ATMOSPHERE WITH NOTHING BUT A FEW INCHES OF METAL AND COMBUSTION MECHANICS SEPARATING YOU FROM THE ELEMENTS?

OH, I THINK I CAN IMAGINE THAT, ALL RIGHT...
...I JUST DON'T KNOW, MR. NKOSI.
THAT'S A WHOLE LOTTA LETTUCE, BUT I'D HAFTA BE INSANE TO TAKE THE JOB!

ALL THE SANE PILOTS TURNED ME DOWN, MR. SECORD.

I SURE AM TEMPTED, MR. NKOSI, BUT I PROMISED MY GIRL--
ALL I ASK IS THAT YOU CONSIDER MY REQUEST.

YOU CAN CONTACT ME HERE IF YOU WANT THE JOB.
MY MAN WILL DRIVE YOU HOME.

MR. SECORD?
LET'S MAKE THE WORLD A BETTER PLACE, SHALL WE?

"SURELY A GOAL WE BOTH CAN BE PROUD TO STRIVE FOR."
SURE, THAT CRAZY PLANE NKOSI COOKED UP COULD TURN ME INTA HAMBURGER, BUT WHAT TEST FLIGHT COULDN'T?
IT'D STILL BEAT FIGHTING NAZIS, RIGHT?

AN HONEST GIG WHERE I COULD ACTUALLY DO SOME GOOD AND MAYBE MAKE BETTY PROUD OF ME, FOR ONCE...
...NOT TA MENTION THE MONEY!
VVVRRROOOM

WHAT THE HELL--
--WHAT'RE THESE CLOWNS TRYIN' TA PULL?!
HEY-- PULL OVER, WOULD YA?

WHAT'S THE BIG IDEA, HUH?
HOOONNK HOOONNK
YOU FELLAS WANNA CHAT?
WELL, HERE I AM!
IF I HAD A PENNY FOR EVERY LOW-RENT, TRENCH COAT-WEARIN' GOON I'VE HAD TA SIDESTEP...!

I GOTTA NIX THESE KINDA SHENANIGANS FOR THE SAKE OF MY FUTURE WITH BETTY.
SOONER OR LATER, SHE'S GONNA BE DONE WITH A BUM LIKE ME.
SAY, KITTEN-- WHADDYA THINK ABOUT YOU AN' ME GOIN' OUT ON THE TOWN TONIGHT?
ROGUE
BERTRAND MODELING AGENCY, LOS ANGELES.
I TOLD YOU--
--I'M NOT INTERESTED.
I CAN REALLY GREASE THE WHEELS FOR YER CAREER...
Simplicity
YOU TALK TO ME LIKE THAT AGAIN AND I'LL PUT OUT YOUR LIGHTS THE HARD WAY.

"ONLY ONE FELLA GETS TO BE WITH ME, AND BOY--
"--YOU SURE AREN'T HIM."
THIS NKOSI GUY ON THE LEVEL?
HUH?
HE'S MAKIN' SERIOUS WAVES ON THE ENGINEERIN' CIRCUIT, THAT'S FER SURE.
THE GREAT INTERNATIONAL AIR RACE

THIS RACE, THOUGH--I'VE HEARD THERE'RE SOME REAL HEAVYWEIGHTS TAKIN' PART.

SOME GERMAN FLIER, "THE IRON BARON" THEY CALL 'IM...
...GEEZ!
I KNOW, PEEV!
I'M GETTING' SQUIRRELLY JUST THINKIN' A' THAT FIRECRACKER HE WANTS ME TA FLY... BUT THIS'D BE HONEST WORK, RIGHT?
YOU SAID YA WANTED ME T'FORGET THE ROCKET!

YEP--AND I ALSO SAID I WANTED YA IN ONE PIECE, TOO!
THIS RACE COULD REALLY PUT ME ON THE MAP AS A BONA FIDE PILOT!

LET ME TEST MYSELF AGAINST THE BEST A' THE BEST!

WHY DOES IT ALWAYS GOTTA BE DEATH OR GLORY WITH YOU, KID, HUH?
IT AIN'T THAT SIMPLE, PEEV.
I GOTTA THINK THIS THROUGH...
TALK TA--

BETTY!
I COULDN'T BELIEVE YOUR CALL!
PARIS!
YOU REALLY HAVE A JOB OFFER THERE?
FOR DELTON NKOSI?
OH, CLIFF, IT'S SO EXCITING!
YEAH, IT'S A PEACH, ALL RIGHT.
TON OF DOUGH, TOO.
I KNOW HOW MUCH YOU WANNA SEE PARIS, AND FOR YER MODELING--
IT'S SO THOUGHTFUL OF YOU TO FIND WORK THAT SUITED MY CAREER, TOO, HONEY!
MAYBE YOU ARE CHANGING!
LISTEN BETTY--IT MIGHT NOT ALL BE SMOOTH SAILING.
THIS IS TEST PILOT STUFF--IT'S UNPREDICTABLE.
I... I JUST DIDN'T WANNA TAKE THE GIG WITHOUT RUNNIN' IT PAST YOU FIRST.
MORE DANGEROUS THAN FLYING AROUND WITH THAT DEATH TRAP STRAPPED TO YOUR BACK?
MORE DANGEROUS THAN CONSTANTLY BEING SHOT AT AND ALMOST GETTING US ALL KILLED?
HECK NO.

COPENHAGEN AIRSTRIP, DENMARK.
"WE'D GET TO SEE EUROPE...
RACE
"WORST THING THAT COULD REALLY HAPPEN WOULD BE THE ODD ENGINE PROBLEM...
The GREAT RACE
"...OR NASTY TURBULENCE.
"SURE, SOME OF THE OTHER PILOTS MAY POSE A REAL CHALLENGE--
"--BUT YOU KNOW WHAT I CAN DO UP THERE. I'D SMOKE 'EM.
"HONESTLY, BETTS...
"...I THINK THIS COULD BE A CINCH."

I'VE GOT TO FIGURE OUT WHAT TO PACK!
I WONDER WHAT THEY'RE WEARING IN PARIS...?
...LOOKS LIKE I'M TAKIN' THE JOB.
LOOKS LIKE.
AH, YA GOT HER BLESSIN', KID-- YER GOLDEN.
LIKE BETTY SAYS, IT SURE BEATS GETTIN' SHOT AT WHILE WEARIN' STOLEN GOVERNMENT PROPERTY.
YEAH!
"WHO'S BETTER IN A STRAIGHT RACE THAN ME, PEEV?"
<YOU UNDERSTAND YOUR ASSIGNMENT, HERR BARON?>
JAWOHL, HERR COLONEL.
<I AM TO RETRIEVE NKOSI'S ROCKET TECHNOLOGY AT ALL COSTS.>
SEHR GUT.

"ALLOW NOBODY TO STAND IN YOUR WAY."
MAYBE IT REALLY IS TIME TO TURN THIS THING IN.
OL' PEEV ADDED A TWO-WAY RADIO TO THE HELMET WHEN HE PATCHED IT UP...
...WHY DOES HE KEEP IMPROVIN' IT IF HE WANTS ME TO QUIT IT?
I REALLY DO NEED MY BRAINS COUNTED--
--KEEPIN' THIS THING AROUND, WHEN IT JUST BRINGS ME GRIEF.
HELLO?
IT'S CLIFF SECORD.
AH, MR. SECORD.
I TRUST YOU'VE HAD AMPLE TIME TO CONSIDER MY OFFER...?
I'M IN, PROFESSOR.
YOU'VE GOT YERSELF A PILOT.

ART BY STEPHEN MOONEY

ART BY GABRIEL RODRÍGUEZ COLORS BY LEN O'GRADY

CHAPLIN AIRDROME, LOS ANGELES.
THIS IS IT, FOLKS!
THE BIGGEST DATE IN THE HISTORY OF THE WORLD AVIATION CALENDAR!
THE BEST AIRPLANES, THE BEST PILOTS-- THE BEST SEATS IN THE HOUSE!
8

The GREAT RAC
STILL NO FURTHER WORD ON WHETHER OR NOT LUCAS BIDSTRUP, THE ACE DANISH PILOT, WILL BE TAKING PART OR, INDEED, AS TO HIS CURRENT WHEREABOUTS!

The GREAT RACE
THE IRISH PILOT, PASCAL "RASCAL" MCGOWAN, HAS ONCE AGAIN BEEN LOCATED AND RESTORED TO HIS PLANE AFTER COMPLETING THE REQUIRED SOBRIETY TESTS.
A REAL CHARACTER, THAT ONE!
RACE OFFICIALS SAY THAT BIDSTRUP ISN'T THE ONLY PILOT YET TO PRESENT FOR FINAL REGISTRATION, BUT I'M SURE WE'LL BE SEEING ALL OF YOUR FAVORITES BEFORE THE STARTING GUN TOMORROW!

SMART MONEY SAYS THAT ANYBODY WITH A REAL STAKE IN THE GAME WILL BE DOING WHATEVER IT TAKES TO WIN THIS ONE!
--NO, YOU STILL HAVE THE IGNITION SEQUENCE INCORRECT--
--YOU CAN'T APPLY ANY THRUST UNTIL THE INITIAL BURNERS HAVE FIRED.
I MEAN--I'M DOIN' WHAT YA TOLD ME TO!
EVIDENTLY YOU ARE NOT.
LET'S TRY IT AGA--
--OH, HELLO, DEAR!
COME TO SEE WHAT THE BOYS ARE MUCKING AROUND WITH?
YOU'RE PLAYING A DANGEROUS GAME.
DARLING, PLEASE--I KNOW WHAT I'M DOING.
SOMETIMES WE MUST LOWER OURSELVES... WITH UNDESIRABLE SORTS, EH?
YA KNOW I'M SITTIN' RIGHT HERE, RIGHT?
HA!
NOT YOU, MY DEAR FELLOW!
NOW DO RUN ALONG, DEAR--
--THE DISCOURSE IS ABOUT TO TAKE A TURN FOR THE TECHNICAL.
YIPES.
STILL WITH ME, SECORD?
NOW REMEMBER--AND THIS IS IMPERATIVE--INITIAL BURNERS FIRST, THEN THRUST!
GIVE IT A TRY!

OKAY, PROF...
BURNERS...
FWOOOOM

...THEN THRUST!
RRRRRRRRR

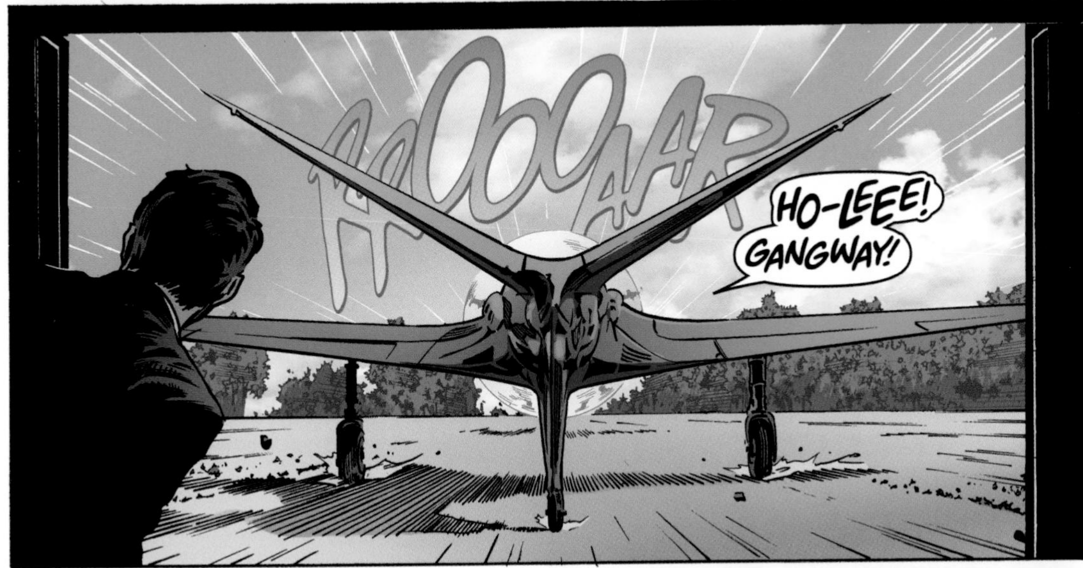
HOOOOAAR
HO-LEEE! GANGWAY!

HOLY SMOKES, THIS THING MOVES.
NKOSI INDUSTRIES
THAT'S THE TICKET!
I'LL SEE YOU AT THE STARTING LINE!

"SURE, IF I MAKE IT THAT FAR!"

EATS

THE BULLDOG CAFÉ.
USUAL, PLEASE, MILLIE.
COMIN' RIGHT UP!
ANYTHING FOR YOU, BETTY?
JUST COFFEE, THANKS, MILLIE.

HMM...?
HI, CAN I ORDER, PLEASE?
WITH YA IN ONE SEC, HON.

HOLY HECK--
--THAT'S DEBBIE SEVILLE!

HMM?
OH, HI!
YOU HERE FOR THE RACE, OL' TIMER?
NAW!
WELL, KINDA--I'M A MECHANIC FOR ONE A' THA OTHER PILOTS.

BUT YOU!
YOU'VE WON IT ALL!
SHE'S WON?!
I DIDN'T REALIZE WOMEN COULD FLY IN THESE RACES!

THAT'LL TEACH ME TO BE MORE OPEN-MINDED--
CLIFF!
YOU'RE HERE!
WHAT'S LEFT A' ME, SURE!
THAT BUGATTI IS NO JOKE--I'M ALL BANGED-UP!
CLIFF--THIS IS THE DEBBIE SEVILLE!
SHE'S HERE FOR THE RACE!
HIYA, CLIFF.
NICE TA MEET ANOTHER CONTESTANT!
CLIFF, YOU SIT HERE BESIDE--
MENU
HEY--
--I'VE HEARD OF YOU AND THE TIMES YOU'VE SET!
I JUST DIDN'T REALIZE YOU'D BE SO--
--FEMALE?
IMPRESSIVE.
ALL RIGHT, BUSTER, KEEP YOUR EYES IN THEIR--
--WHOA!

WHAT A CHARMING CAFÉ!
MAY WE PLEASE SEE A MEN--
--OH!
PARDON ME, MA'AM.
OH, SORRY!

THE FAULT LIES ENTIRELY WITH ME, CLUMSY OAF THAT I AM.
BUT YOU!
WHAT AN EXQUISITE CREATURE YOU ARE!

?!
HEY--SLOW YER ROLL, PAL.
AH! A FELLOW PILOT!
YOU SHALL BE TAKING PART IN THE GREAT RACE?

YOU BET YER SWEET BIPPY I AM!
AN' I'LL BE WINNIN' IT, TOO!

SUCH CONFIDENCE!
WE'LL SEE.

A TRAIT AS AMERICAN AS THE APPLE PIE, EH, BOYS?
HEY! GET YOUR DAMN--

MY APOLOGIES, THAT WAS RUDE.
IT WAS NOT MY INTENTION TO TAKE THAT WHICH IS YOURS.

MENU
OH, YER CRUISIN' FOR A BRUISIN' NOW, FRITZ!
MAKING FRIENDS ALREADY, BARON?
NEVER DOES TAKE YOU LONG.
HAVEN'T SEEN YOU SINCE THOSE TEST FLIGHTS IN COLOGNE IN '36.
DEBORAH!
FINALLY, SOME TRUE COMPETITION!
ONLY MY PA CALLS ME THAT, MISTER.
MAYBE YOU SHOULD LET THESE PEOPLE EAT IN PEACE?

YOU ARE CORRECT, OF COURSE!
MY MOST SINCERE APOLOGIES, MA'AM.

I TEND TO GET AHEAD OF MYSELF AND OFTEN AHEAD OF OTHERS.

GOOD DAY, EVERYONE!
I SHALL SEE YOU ON THE STARTING LINE.
AND MAY THE BEST MAN WIN!

INSUFFERABLE BASTARD.
SOMETHING UNCOMFORTABLY FAMILIAR ABOUT THAT BIG LUG, BUT I CAN'T QUITE PLACE IT...

BOY, THAT DEBBIE SURE IS A FORCE A' NATURE, HUH?
SHE SURE TOOK THE WIND OUTTA THAT TWIT'S SAILS.
1153
45¢ QT
25¢ PT
5¢
!
DIDN'T I TELL YA?
SHE'S SOMETHIN' ELSE.
HE WASN'T SO BAD.
AT LEAST HE HAD MANNERS.
HUH?
THE GUY WAS A TOTAL CRUMB!
SAME OLD CLIFF, QUICK TO JUDGE ANYTHING HE DOESN'T UNDERSTAND!
YA LOST ME, BETTS.
I THOUGHT--
LEAVE IT--SHE'S JUST STEAMED ABOUT DEBBIE.
DEBBIE?
WHY?
AH, BETTY'S JUST USED TO BEIN' THE MAIN ATTRACTION ROUND THESE PARTS.
SHE'LL BE FINE ONCE SHE CALMS DOWN.
YA WEREN'T KIDDIN', KID--
--THIS THING'S A BEAUT.
LOTTA COMPONENTS I DON'T RECOGNIZE...
...THIS NKOSI FELLER MIGHT JUST BE AS SMART AS THE PAPERS SAY HE IS.
WITH ALL THE FUEL SHE'S CARRYIN', THOUGH, AN' WHAT LOOKS TA BE A COMPLETE LACK A' THE STANDARD CUTOFFS AN' SAFETIES...
...THIS THING IS ABOUT AS CLOSE TO A ROCKET AS THAT DANGED PACK.

"SPEAKIN' A WHICH--
"--YA NEVER DID TELL ME HOW YA GOT OUTTA THAT SCRAPE IN RUSTIC CANYON?
"HOW COME YA AIN'T FLAT AS A PANCAKE?"
"WELL, THE KRAUTS HAD VENTILATED THE ROCKET--
"--BUT THE ROCKETEER WASN'T LICKED YET!"
GOTTA SLOW MY DESCENT!
IF THIS DOESN'T WORK--
--I'M
HAMBURGER-RAAAGHHH!
THUK
KRAK
THIS IS IT--
--MALIBOU LAKE!
SNAP
SPLOOSH

HOO BOY.
EVEN BY MY STANDARDS, THAT WAS DAMN LUC--

--HUH?
VOICES?
GERMAN VOICES!

<THIS WAY-->*
<--I SWEAR I HEARD SOMETHING!>
<CHECK IT!>
*TRANSLATED FROM GERMAN.

<HALF RATIONS FOR ANY MAN THAT DOESN'T FIND SOMETHING!>
?!

<NOTHING, SIR.>
<IF HE WAS THERE-->

<--HE HAS ESCAPED.>
<FINALLY.>
<SOME TRUE COMPETITION.>

THE MORNING OF THE RACE.
The GREAT RACE

--FELLOWS, YOU HAVEN'T SEEN ANYTHING YET.
SURE, SOME OF THESE FOREIGN FLIERS HAVE REAL SKILL AND KNOW HOW TO HANDLE THOSE MACHINES.
BUT SKILL CAN ONLY TAKE YOU SO FAR IN THE FACE OF TRUE REVOLUTION.
MY NKOSI 5000 WILL REWRITE THE RECORD BOOKS.
SHE'LL PEN A TUNE THAT YOU'LL ALL BE HUMMING, COME THIS TIME TOMORROW.

WHAT ABOUT YOUR PILOT, PROFESSOR?
SHOULD WE HAVE HEARD OF THIS SECORD GUY?
WHAT PREVIOUS RACES HAS HE WON?
PRESS

CLIFF SECORD WON THE RACE TO FLY MY PLANE, GENTLEMEN.
NOBODY CAN FLY LIKE THIS PILOT, AND THAT'S WHY HE'S WORKING FOR ME.

MS. ASSUAGE, COULD YOU TELL US--
I--
WE'D LOVE TO STAY AND CHAT, FELLAS, BUT I'M NEEDED AT MY PLANE.
I'LL SEE YOU BOYS IN LONDON!
MS. ASSUAGE!
PRESS
PROFESSOR!
PROFESSOR NKOSI!

ACROSS THE AIRFIELD...
WOULDYA LOOKIT THESE MACHINES, PEEV?
CAN YA IMAGINE THE PRICE TAG FER SOMETHIN' LIKE THAT?
COST AIN'T EVERYTHIN', KID--
--IT'S TUNIN' AN' MAINTENANCE THAT COUNT.

YOU TELL 'IM, MR. PEEVY!
DEBBIE!
FWEET
SHE'S A STUNNER!
YEAH, AND THE AIRPLANE AIN'T BAD EITHER, RIGHT, PEEV?

YER PACKIN' THAT NEW TWIN-CYLINDER FUEL INJECTION SYSTEM, HUH?
HEY, YA REALLY KNOW YER STUFF, MR. PEEVY!
AW, IT AIN'T NUTHIN' ANY HALFWAY-DECENT ENGINEER WOULDN'T KNOW. AND IT'S PEEVY, NO "MISTER."

YOU GUYS SCOPIN' OUT THE COMPETITION?
MIND IF I JOIN YA?

HEY, NICE WORK, ROMEO!
STOW IT, YOU!
I'M OLD ENOUGH TA BE HER GRANPAPPY!

I'VE FLOWN AGAINST SOME OF THESE GUYS BEFORE.
THE JAPANESE PILOT AND THE ITALIAN.
BOTH FORMER WORLD-RECORD HOLDERS.
I DOUBT YOU'VE EVER HAD TO COMPETE WITH ANYONE ON THEIR LEVEL, CLIFF.
OH YEAH?
WELL, THEY'VE NEVER RACED ANYONE LIKE ME BEFORE, NEITHER.
THAT'S THE SPIRIT, FLYBOY!
SOMETHING TELLS ME THEY HAVEN'T.

RACE
COFFEE
STATION
RTICIPANTS
ONLY
SUGAR
CLIFF!
HIYA, BETTS!
AIN'T THIS ALL SOMETHIN'?
IT'S ALL SO GLAMOROUS!
I THINK I SAW THE GOVERNOR!
SO YER SQUARE ON THE PLAN?
YOU'LL MEET ME AT THE HOTEL IN PARIS?
HOW COULD I FORGET-- I'M SO EXCITED!
YOU PROMISE TO BE CAREFUL?

IT'S ALL COPACETIC, BETTY-- PROMISE.
GOOD MORNING, MS. BETTY!
WHAT A STUNNINGLY BEAUTIFUL WOMAN YOU ARE.
AND, LOOK, SECORD IS HERE, TOO.
COME TO TAKE A LOOK AT YOUR FELLOW PILOTS, EH?
I GOTTA ADMIT, THAT IS ONE CHERRY RIDE YA GOT.

ISN'T SHE?
HOLDER OF SEVERAL GLOBAL AIRSPEED RECORDS AND SPECIALLY MODIFIED FOR LONG-DISTANCE FLIGHT.
I DARESAY YOU DON'T STAND A CHANCE, SIR!
YEAH, WELL, YOU'LL SEE JUST WHAT I DARE SOON ENOUGH.

SAY, BETTS--
--HELP ME OUT AN' BUTTER THE BARON'S BISCUIT A LITTLE, COULD YA?
CLIFF!
YOU ARE SUCH A CHILD SOMETIMES!
YER THE BEST, HONEY!
SIGH.
SO IMPRESSIVE!
DO YOU THINK I COULD TAKE A RIDE IN YOUR PLANE SOMETIME?
AH, FRÄULEIN!
WOULD THAT YOU COULD.
ALAS, NOBODY FLIES IN THIS MACHINE BUT ME.
BUT I POSSESS SEVERAL AUTOMOBILES THAT MAY TAKE YOUR FANCY.
ALL FROM STERLING GERMAN MANUFACTURERS, OF COURSE.
OH, OF COURSE.
SUGAR
LET'S SEE YER STERLING GERMAN MANUFACTURING COPE WITH THIS.
RIGHT-O, HONEY--BEST IF WE HEAD ON AND GET READY--THE RACE IS ONLY A COUPLE HOURS OFF.
I'LL SEE YOU IN THE SKIES, PAL.
I LOOK FORWARD TO IT!
JA.
HE IS HEADING TOWARD NKOSI'S MACHINE NOW.

I REALLY WOULD APPRECIATE IT IF YOU DIDN'T TAMPER WITH MY PLANE QUITE SO MUCH, MR. PEEVY.
WHILE YOU ARE UNDOUBTEDLY AN ENGINEER OF EXCEPTIONAL ABILITY, THIS MACHINE REQUIRES SOMEWHAT OF A MORE REFINED TOUCH.
JUST MAKIN' SURE YER MACHINE DOESN'T REFINE CLIFF INTO HIS CONSTITUENT PARTS, MR. NKOSI.

SCOPE THIS, PEEV--I FILLED THAT BARON FELLA'S GAS TANK FULLA SUGAR!
CLIFF, YA MAROON--THAT'S A MYTH!
IT WON'T DO NOTHIN' BUT SETTLE ON THE BOTTOM!

WHAT?!
IT ALWAYS WORKED IN THA LOONEY TUNES!
THERE'S THAT CLASSICAL EDUCATION COMIN' INTA PLAY AGAIN.
DANG IT.

GUESS YOU'LL JUST HAFTA WHUP THIS KRAUT THE OL' FASHIONED WAY, KID.
GIVE 'EM HELL!
I COULD USE A KISS FER LUCK, LADY!
MWAH

PILOTS--TO YOUR AIRPLANES!
SEE YA IN PARIS, BETTY!
PARIS!

YOU READIN' ME, PROF?
LOUD AND CLEAR, SECORD.
ALL YOUR LEVELS ARE NORMAL AND IN THE GREEN.
TIME TO SHOW THEM WHAT OUR BIRD CAN DO.
THE PLANES WILL LAUNCH IN STAGGERED WAVES SO AS NOT TO CLUTTER THE RACEWAY!
VVRRRMMMMMMMMMM
YES, SIR, ROGER THAT!
I'LL SEE YOU BOZOS IN LONDON!
AND THEY'RE OFF!
THE IRON BARON TAKES AN UNORTHODOX LINE--
WHAT'S THAT LUNATIC DOIN'--?
HE'S GONNA FORCE--
OH MY, IF HE'S NOT CAREFUL--
HOLY SMOKES!
KRASH
HE TOOK THAT POOR SAP RIGHT OUT!
HIS METHODS MAY BE BRUTAL, BUT YOU CAN'T ARGUE WITH HIS RESULTS, SECORD.
RROOAAARRRR
YOUR CONCERN FOR MY WELL-BEIN' IS REAL TOUCHIN', PROF.
HE IS THE PILOT TO BEAT-- WHATEVER IT TAKES.

THE AUSTRALIAN FLIER IS DOWN!
HELPED IN NO SMALL MEASURE BY THE DANGEROUS TACTICS EMPLOYED BY THE GERMAN PILOT!
GOOD HEAVENS--WHAT HAPPENED?
IS THAT PILOT ALL RIGHT?!
YER PAL THE BARON HAPPENED.
CLIFF IS IN FOR A REAL HUMDINGER WITH THIS ONE.
CLIFF SAID IT WAS JUST A RACE!
WELL, I MEAN, TECHNICALLY, IT IS--
--SOME FOLK JUS' DON'T PLAY FAIR.
REMEMBER THE PLAN, SECORD.
SLOW AND STEADY--SO TO SPEAK.
WHEN THE CORRECT TIME COMES, WE SHALL OVERTAKE THE BARON.
I'LL DO MY BEST, PROF.
SOMETHING TELLS ME I MAY HAVE TA... IMPROVISE A LITTLE.
NEGATIVE, SECORD!
THE ENTIRE DISTANCE AND DURATION OF THE FLIGHT PLAN IS MEASURED TO THE CLOSEST FRACTION AGAINST OUR FUEL LOGISTICS!
OKAY, OKAY--I GOT IT.
STICK TO THE PLAN.
THE RACE IS UNDERWAY.
OUR AGENT IN THE FIELD WILL REPORT IN AT THE EARLIEST OPPORTUNITY.
WE SHALL MAKE HASTE FOR NEW YORK AND THEN ON TO ENGLAND, AS PLANNED.

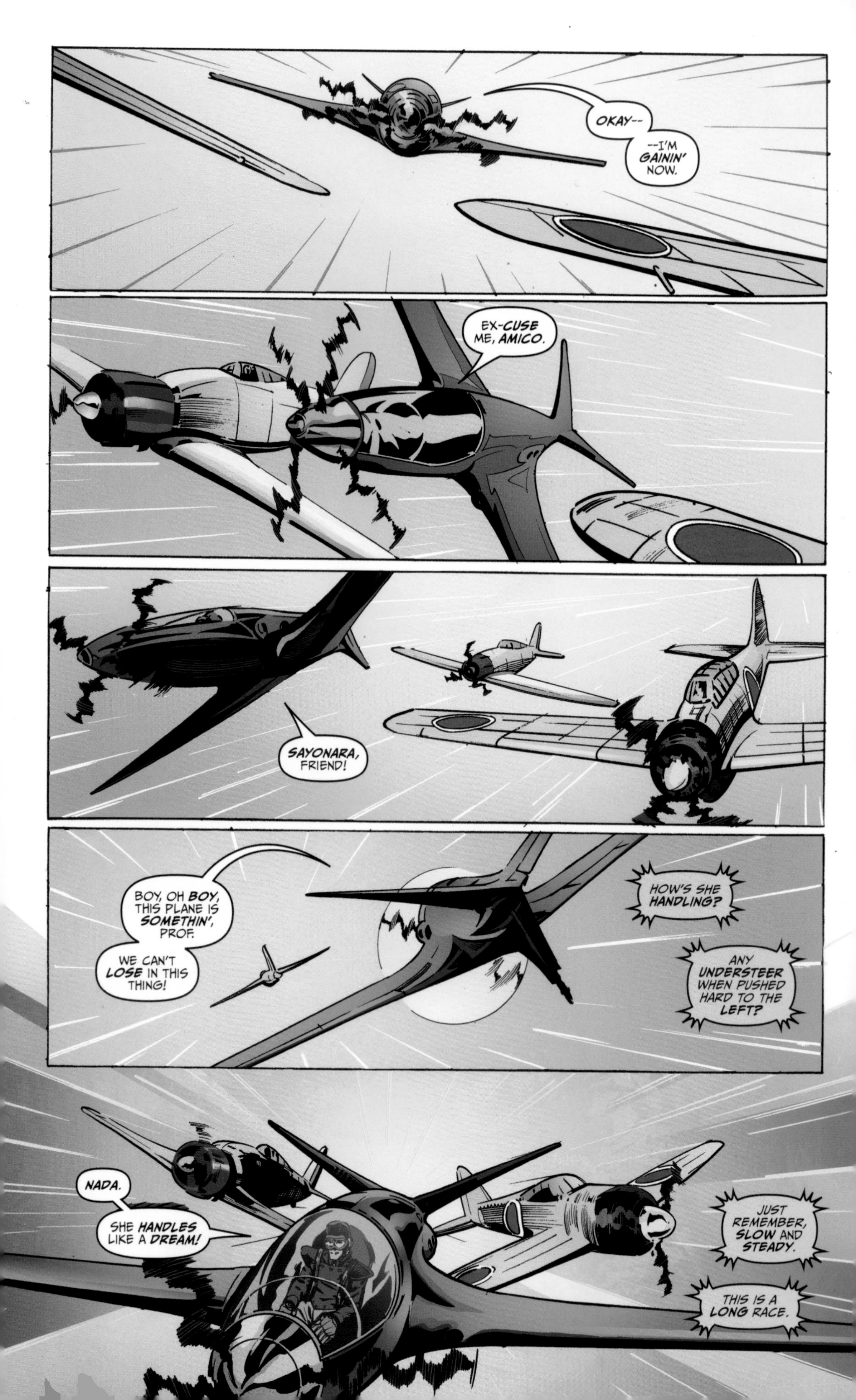
OKAY--
--I'M GAININ' NOW.
EX-CUSE ME, AMICO.
SAYONARA, FRIEND!
BOY, OH BOY, THIS PLANE IS SOMETHIN', PROF.
WE CAN'T LOSE IN THIS THING!
HOW'S SHE HANDLING?
ANY UNDERSTEER WHEN PUSHED HARD TO THE LEFT?
NADA.
SHE HANDLES LIKE A DREAM!
JUST REMEMBER, SLOW AND STEADY.
THIS IS A LONG RACE.

HOURS LATER.
NEW YORK.
APPROACHING THE FUEL STOP NOW, PROF.
HOW WE LOOKIN'?
WE'RE IN GOOD SHAPE, SECORD.
SECOND PLACE BEHIND THE GERMAN, EXACTLY AS I PLANNED.
YOU SHOULD PROBABLY KNOW THAT THE RACE AUTHORITIES LOST CONTACT WITH THE SWISS FLIER SOMEWHERE OVER NEBRASKA...
...BUT I'M SURE HE'S FINE.
OH. I'M SURE.
HE'S PROBABLY JUST TAKIN' THE SCENIC ROUTE.
OR, MORE LIKELY, HE FLEW INTO SOME ROUGH AIR, COURTESY OF OUR FRIEND THE BARON!
SAY, HOW FAR AHEAD IS THE FIRST PLANE?
THE BIG GERMAN FELLA?
HE PASSED THROUGH AROUND FIFTEEN MINUTES BACK.
BARELY A HAIR OUTTA PLACE!
SWELL.
JUICE HER UP PRONTO, BOYS--SHE'S A THIRSTY ONE!
AIRPORT
SERVICE
AN' HERE WAS ME THINKIN' I WAS MAKIN' GREAT TIME!
GOTTA GIVE 'ER ALL SHE'S GOT!

SECORD!
SLOW DOWN, DAMMIT!
YOU'LL BURN OFF YOUR FUEL TOO QUICKLY!
DON'T WORRY, PROF. I KNOW WHAT I'M DOING!
I'M TOO FAR BEHIND, GOTTA CLOSE THE GAP!
SECORD, YOU IDIOT-- I EXPLAINED THIS!
THAT SPECIAL FUEL BLEND NEEDS TO BE MIXED AND INJECTED ONLY AT SPECIFIED INTERVALS!
YOU'RE RISKING YOUR LIFE AND MY PRIZE!
WITH ALL DUE RESPECT, PROF, YOU'RE THE SCIENCE WHIZ AN' I'M THE PILOT--
--THIS IS WHY YOU HIRED ME. JUST TRUST ME TO DO MY JOB.

HOURS LATER...
I DID IT!
I KNEW I COULD CATCH THIS GUY!

I DUNNO WHAT THE PROF WAS WORRIED ABOU--
KOFF SPUTTER
UH-OH!
UM, I GOTTA REAL SITUATION HERE, PROF!
LOSING SPEED AND ALTITUDE!

PROF!
I'M GOIN' DOWN!

ART BY STEPHEN MOONEY COLORS BY IAN FAY

ART BY GABRIEL RODRÍGUEZ COLORS BY LEN O'GRADY

MAYDAY, MAYDAY!
I'M GOIN' DOWN!
PROF?!
TALK TA ME!
HEYA, FLYBOY!
YOU SURE HAVE A FLAIR FOR THE DRAMATIC, I'LL GIVE YA THAT!
DEBBIE?!
BOY, AM I GLAD TA SEE YOU!
THINGS'RE LOOKIN' A MITE HAIRY FER ME RIGHT NOW--
--I'M LOSIN' ALTITUDE FAST!
WHAT'S THE PROBLEM?
OUTTA GAS!
YOU GOTTA BE KIDDIN' ME!
I'M GONNA DROP DOWN RIGHT OVER YA--THERE'S AN AUXILIARY TANK UNDER MY FUSELAGE!
MATCH MY SPEED EXACTLY OR WE'RE BOTH SUNK!

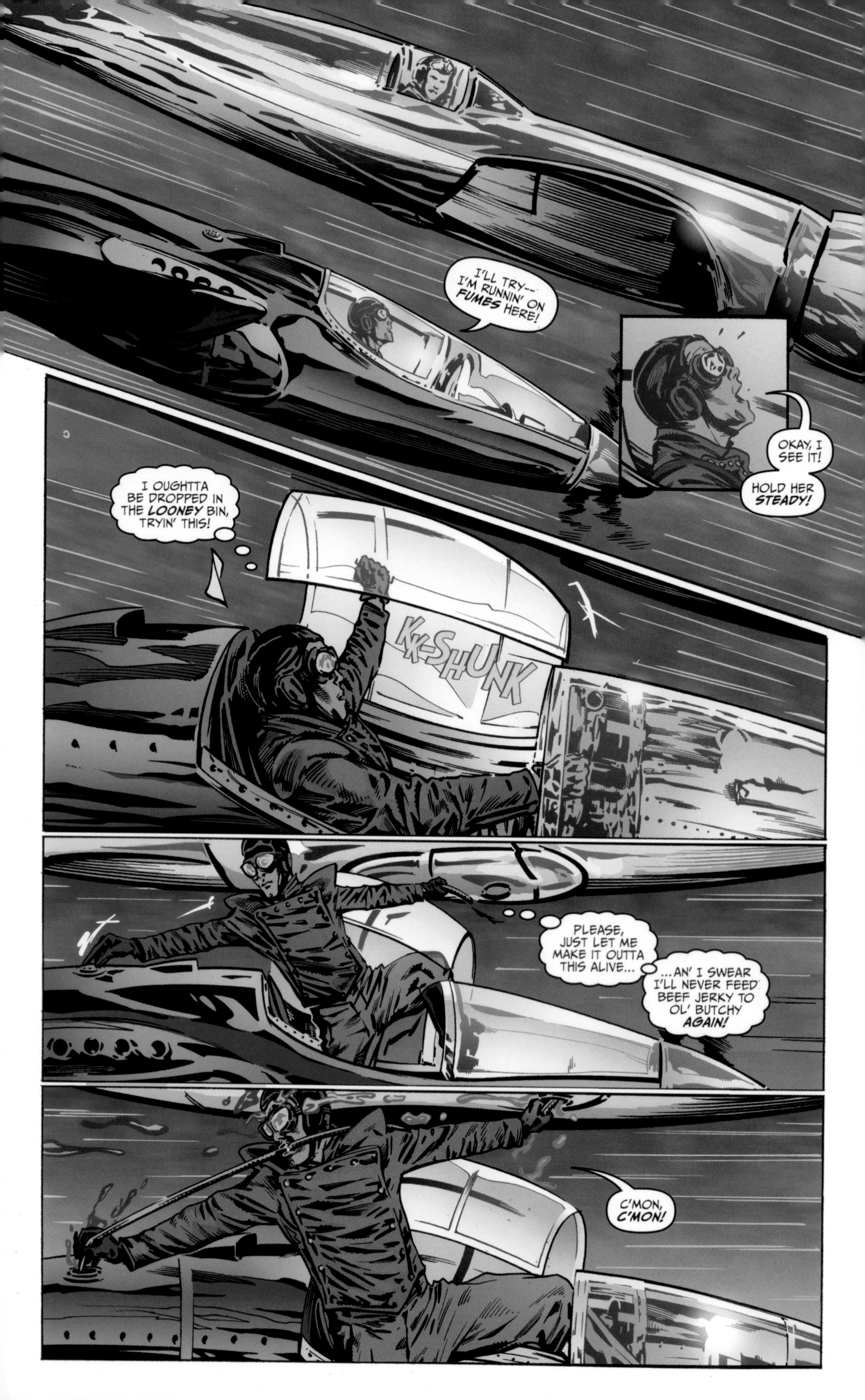
I'LL TRY-- I'M RUNNIN' ON FUMES HERE!
OKAY, I SEE IT!
HOLD HER STEADY!
I OUGHTTA BE DROPPED IN THE LOONEY BIN, TRYIN' THIS!
KK-SHUNK
PLEASE, JUST LET ME MAKE IT OUTTA THIS ALIVE...
...AN' I SWEAR I'LL NEVER FEED BEEF JERKY TO OL' BUTCHY AGAIN!
C'MON, C'MON!

TENSE MINUTES LATER...
THAT'LL HAFTA SEE ME TO LONDON--
--I'M OUTTA TIME!
CAREFUL...
WHUMP
WHOOEEE!
WE DID IT, DEBBIE!
REMIND ME NEVER TO TELL BETTY ABOUT THAT ONE!
CLUNK
GLAD TA HEAR IT, FLYBOY!
FIRST BEER IN LONDON'S ON YOU!
A-MEN TO THAT, SISTER.
SECORD?
SECORD?!
WHAT THE HELL HAVE YOU DONE TO MY PLANE?!
YEAH, I'M FINE, PROF, THANKS.
IF YOU'VE DAMAGED--
PLANE'S FINE, PROF.
SHE JUST NEEDS A GOOD DRINK.
KNOW JUST HOW SHE FEELS...
WE EVEN MADE UP SOME TIME ON THE BARON.

LONDON, ENGLAND.
REGIONAL A
THIS ISN'T RESOLVED, SECORD.
REPORT IN AS SOON AS YOU GET TO--
BE GOOD TO HER, FELLAS. IT WAS A BUMPY ONE.
NKOSI WANTS A DEBRIEF, SECORD.
YEAH, YEAH.
NKOSI
AH, MR. SECORD.
THIRD FLOOR, WITH THE REST OF THE CONTESTANTS.
YOU'RE IN ROOM 22.
'PRECIATE IT, BUD, THANKS.
HOTEL SHALVÉ
MR. SECORD, MR. NKOSI LEFT A NUMBER FOR YOU. HE REQUESTED YOU CALL HIM RIGHT AWAY. THERE IS A GUEST PHONE JUST TO YOUR RIGHT.
HEY, BOSS.
I WANTED TO APOLOGIZE--
--YOU WERE RIGHT, I PUSHED HER TOO HARD, TOO FAST.
WELL, ACCORDING TO MY ENGINEERS, IT SEEMS THAT NO LASTING DAMAGE WAS DONE.
BUT LEARN FROM THIS, SECORD.
I KNOW MY PLANE BETTER THAN ANYONE, INCLUDING YOU!
IT MIGHT BEHOOVE YOU TO LISTEN TO ME IN THE FUTURE.
ROGER THAT, PROF.
IT WON'T HAPPEN AGAIN.
VERY GOOD, SECORD, SEE THAT IT DOESN'T--
KLIK
YOU GOTTA BE KIDDIN' ME. ARE THOSE--?!
NAW, YER LOSIN' IT, SECORD.

"NOT EVERY JOE IN A LONG COAT IS OUT TA GET YOU AND YOURS."
ONE OF THE FIRST PAN-AMERICAN TRANSATLANTIC OVERNIGHT FLIGHTS.
I SURE HOPE CLIFF IS OKAY.
WORRY AS I MIGHT, THOUGH--
--I CAN'T HELP BUT BE EXCITED!
WE'RE FINALLY GOING TO SEE PARIS!
Die Welt
AND CLIFF IS FLYING AN AIRPLANE, EVEN IF IT IS EXPERIMENTAL, AND NOT THAT CURSED ROCKET PACK.
I TRUST HIM AND I BELIEVE HIM WHEN HE SAYS IT ISN'T ANYTHING HE CAN'T HANDLE.
WHAT'S THE WORST THAT COULD HAPPEN?

THE WALDORF HOTEL, LONDON.
DARLING, I SIMPLY DON'T HAVE TIME FOR THIS RIGHT--
YOU HAVE NO TIME FOR ME, BUT PLENTY FOR THOSE... ANIMALS!

I HAVE TOLD YOU REPEATEDLY--
--IT IS NOT THAT STRAIGHTFORWARD!
THIS IS NOT SOME SIMPLE MORALITY PLAY!
SLAP!
MISTER, YOU KNOW NOTHING ABOUT MORALS.
WE'RE THROUGH!
THIS IS ABOUT SAVING THE WORLD, BELLA!
YOU KEEP TELLING YOURSELF THAT, DELTON.
SUCH AN UTTER LACK OF COMPRE-HENSION...

MY APOLOGIES, GENTLEMEN.
NOW... SHALL WE COMMENCE NEGOTIATIONS?
KLIK

...CUTAWAY COAT, PERFECT FITS...
...PUTTIN' ON THE RITZ!

OW!
WHOK

EVEN WHEN IT'S HIDDEN AWAY, THIS THING BRINGS ME NUTHIN' BUT PAIN.
SO WHY THE HECK DID I EVEN BRING IT ALONG...?

KNOK KNOK
COMING!

SORRY, FLYBOY--
--DIDN'T MEAN TA CATCH YA IN THE ALTOGETHER.

MEET YA DOWN AT THE BAR IN A BIT FER SOME GRUB AN' A DRINK?
762
DOWN IN TEN.

AHOY!
SO, WAS THE OWNER OF YOUR PLANE SORE?
HE SURE WASN'T HAPPY, BUT HONESTLY, I THOUGHT HE'D TAKE IT WORSE.
I WAS EXPECTING BOTH BARRELS, BUT IT WAS MORE OF A "SHAPE UP AN' FLY STRAIGHT" KINDA THING.
GRAVY!
THAT NKOSI CHARACTER SURE IS A WEIRD ONE...
LISTEN, DEBBIE--
--THANKS FOR THE SAVE BACK THERE.
I WAS IN A TIGHT SPOT.
DON'T MENTION IT--'TWEREN'T NUTHIN'.
GOOD THING YOU'RE A CHATTY GUY AND GAVE ME YOUR RADIO FREQUENCY!
SERIOUSLY, THAT WAS ONE A' THE SNAZZIEST PIECES OF AERIAL ACROBATICS I'VE EVER SEEN.
I DIDN'T REALLY THINK ABOUT IT--I JUST KNEW I HAD TO SAVE YOU.
YOU KNOW WHAT?
I KNOW EXACTLY WHAT YA MEAN.
CHEERS.
AH, MY FELLOW PACE-SETTERS!

I AM QUITE IMPRESSED THAT YOU MADE IT THIS FAR, SECORD.
WHEN LAST I SAW YOU, YOU LOOKED TO BE IN SOME... DISTRESS.
OH YEAH?
FUNNY, YOU DIDN'T SEEM TOO CONCERNED AT THE TIME.

SUCH UTTER DISREGARD FOR AN INCREDIBLY VISIONARY PIECE OF TECHNOLOGY!
WHAT WAS THE GREAT NKOSI THINKING IN HIRING YOU?

I'M NOT THE ONE WHO NEEDS TO CHEAT TO WIN, PAL.
TELL ME... WAS THAT EGO STANDARD-ISSUE IN DER LUFTWAFFE?
ALL RIGHT, FELLAS, LET'S TAKE IT DOWN A NOTCH.

AH, AND LITTLE DEBORAH--
--STILL TRYING TO PROVE SHE BELONGS WITH THE BOYS.
I AIN'T RISING TO YOUR LOUSY BAIT, BARON.
LEAVE HER ALONE, JERK!

THIS MAKES ME WONDER...
...WHAT IN THE WORLD IS A WOMAN LIKE BETTY DOING WITH A PATHETIC IDIOT LIKE YOU?
THAT'S IT!
WHAMM
HRRFF!

YOU'VE DONE IT NOW, FLYBOY!
YAAHHH!
HE HAD IT COMIN', DEB!
KRAK
DUCK!
NOW, SECORD.
LET US SEE IF YOU FIGHT AS POORLY AS YOU FLY!
SLAM
OOOF!
WHAK
NORMALLY MESELF AN' THE SWISS BOYO WOULD BE STAYIN' NEUTRAL IN A SCRAP--
AARGH!
HOOFF!
SLAM
KRUNCH

HOOOF!
CRUNCH
KSHH
AARGH!
RRRRRR
WHOA, WHOA--LET'S NOT WRECK THE WHOLE--
WHAM!
EXIT
WHO THREW THE FIRST PUNCH?
AH... I GUESS I DID.
NO HARM DONE, AND NOTHING MORE TO SAY, OFFICER.
JUST A FEW RACERS BLOWING OFF SOME STEAM.
I AM MORE THAN HAPPY TO PAY FOR ANY DAMAGES INCURRED, WITH A FORMAL APOLOGY TO THE PROPRIETOR OF THIS FINE ESTABLISHMENT.

HAHA, THE LOOK ON THAT BIG LUG'S FACE WHEN YA SOCKED HIM--
PRICELESS!
HA--NOT AS IMPRESSIVE AS THIS SHINER I'LL BE SPORTIN' COME MORNIN'!
THIS IS ME-- WHOOP!
EASY THERE!
HAHA...
LISTEN, DEB, YOU'RE A SWELL GIRL, BUT I GOTTA PUT THE BRAKES ON.
HUH?
YEAH, I'M REAL SORRY, BUT ME AN' BETTY HAVE A HECK OF A GOOD THING GOIN', AN' I AIN'T WILLIN' TA RISK THAT, NO MATTER HOW TEMPTIN' IT MIGHT BE.
CLIFF...
I HOPE YA AIN'T SORE AT ME...
BWAHAHAHA!
I...
...I'M CONFUSED.
I AIN'T SORE. PROMISE.
LET'S JUST SAY, YOU AIN'T MY TYPE.
AN' I CAN SEE WHY YER SO NUTS ABOUT BETTY.
HELL, SHE'S GORGEOUS.
OH--
--OH.
SORRY ABOUT--
NOTHIN' T' BE SORRY ABOUT, FLYBOY.
YOU DID REAL GOOD DOWN THERE.
NOW, BETTER HIT THE HAY. BIG DAY TOMORROW.
ACED IT AGAIN, SECORD.

VILLENEUVE-ORLY AIRPORT, PARIS, FRANCE.
"CRIPES, IF BETTY COULD SEE ME NOW..."
OH--IT'S JUST AS BEAUTIFUL AS IT LOOKS IN THE MOVIES!
PARIS - ORLY
15 BK 84

TAXI, S'IL VOUS PLAIT!

MERCI!

IN YOU GO, FRÄULEIN!
HEY!

LET GO--

AARGH!
WHAMM

VERE DID SHE--?!

SOON!
HOTEL DANIEL
MERCI--MERCI BEAUCOUP!
WHY IS IT ALWAYS SOMETHING?
THEY HAD GERMAN ACCENTS, CALLED ME FRÄULEIN... MORE NAZIS?
OH, CLIFF... WHAT HAVE YOU GOTTEN US INTO NOW?
ONE THING IS FOR CERTAIN--
--THAT IS THE LAST TIME SOME GOON TRIES TO BUNDLE ME INTO THE BACK OF SOME DOGGONE CRATE!
TIME TO GET INTO MY ROOM AND BARRICADE THE DOOR UNTIL CLIFF ARRIVES.
THEN WE CAN FIGURE THIS OUT, TOGETH--
KRAK
BE CAREFUL, HONEY--
--THOSE HEELS ARE SHARP!

NEXT MORNING.
AFTER YOUR QUOTES IN CALIFORNIA, YOU CAN'T BE TOO THRILLED WITH THE IRON BARON STEALING YOUR THUNDER.
MY DEAR FELLOW, WE'RE PRECISELY WHERE WE MEAN TO BE.
THE BARON IS A FORMIDABLE PILOT, YES, BUT HE ISN'T FLYING IN MY MACHINE AND SHALL ULTIMATELY LOSE.
BIGGIN HILL AIRSTRIP, LONDON.
I HAVE A PLAN, IT IS IN MOTION, AND ALL IS GOING SWIMMINGLY.
IT WAS ALMOST LITERALLY GOING SWIMMING WHEN SECORD NEARLY DITCHED YOUR PLANE IN THE NORTH ATLANTIC. CARE TO COMMENT?
MERELY KEEPING THINGS INTERESTING FOR YOU LOT!
SAUCE FOR THE GOOSE!
"MY MAN SECORD HAS THE SO-CALLED BARON FIRMLY IN HIS SIGHTS!"
AS PER THE RULES, THE BARON IS PERMITTED A 20-MINUTE HEAD START DUE TO HIS FIRST-PLACE FINISH IN THE PREVIOUS LEG!
EACH ADDITIONAL FLIER WILL BE STAGGERED BASED ON THEIR ARRIVAL TIMES YESTERDAY!
THERE HE GOES, THE ARROGANT BUM.
YOU THINK WE CAN CATCH HIM?
I THINK WE CAN BEAT HIM.
AND WHAT THEN?
WHO WINS?
LET'S JUST CONCENTRATE ON MAKING IT TO THE FINISH LINE IN ONE PIECE.
THEN WE CAN FIGURE OUT WHO'S REALLY THE FASTEST.
LET'S SEE HOW EASY I GO ON YOU, YA MEAN.
VERY WELL.
YOUR PRICE IS ACCEPTABLE.
YOU MAY PUT YOUR PLAN IN MOTION.
BUT WIN OR LOSE, THAT TROPHY GOES TO ME.

THE TWO AMERICAN CONTESTANTS ARE UNDERWAY!
DEBBIE SEVILLE, WHO MOST FANS WILL BE FAMILIAR WITH, AND THE SURPRISE CHALLENGER, CLIFF SECORD!
IT'S ANYBODY'S RACE!
CLIFF SECORD.
HUH?
WHO THE HELL IS THIS?
HOW DID YOU--?
ONLY NKOSI KNOWS THIS FREQUENCY!
WE HAFF YOUR VOMAN.
BETTY?!
YOU VILL FLY THE NKOSI 5000 TO BERLIN, NOT PARIS.
OR SHE VILL DIE.
WAIT--
--WHAT THE HELL ARE YOU TALKING ABOUT?
BZZT
GONE!
PROF!
NKOSI-- DID YOU HEAR THAT?
KLIK KLIK
WHERE THE HELL IS HE?
WAS THAT FOR REAL?!
HOW'D THE KRAUTS GET THE FREQUENCY OF OUR CREW CHANNEL?
HOW WOULD THEY EVEN KNOW WHERE BETTY WAS GONNA BE?
CHANGE COURSE NOW AND I LOSE THE RACE!
BUT IF BETTY REALLY IS IN DANGER...

SOMEWHERE NEAR THE FRENCH COAST.
APOLOGIES, SECORD, I HAD TO STEP OUT FOR A MOMENT.
ARE YOU THERE, SECORD?
SECORD?!
TIME TO SEE WHAT THIS CRAZY FUEL BLEND OF HIS CAN REALLY DO.
WOOAAHHH!
I'M COMIN', BETTY!
FWOOOOSH

JA... SHE IS COOPERATING.
NO TROUBLE SO FAR.
OH, I'LL GIVE YOU BOYS SOME TROUBLE...
ASK THEM IF THEY VANT US TO MOTIVATE SECORD A LITTLE.
MAYBE VE TAKE A FINGER?
HOTEL LUTETIA, PARIS.

WHOK
HNNHH!

VAS--
KRASH
I SWEAR--THE NEXT MAN THAT TRIES TO TIE ME UP WILL GET MORE THAN A KICK IN THE FACE!

MORE OF THEM... FELLAS, YOU PICKED THE WRONG GIRL TO KIDNAP!
KSHH
!

KLONG
OWW!

WHAT THE HELL, BETTS?
I'M HERE TA RESCUE YOU!

DO I LOOK LIKE I NEED RESCUING?
WELL, NO, BUT I THOUGHT--
I HIT YOU BECAUSE I THOUGHT YOU WERE ONE OF THEM.

HOW DID YOU KNOW WHERE TO FIND ME?
I FIGURED I'D TRY YER HOTEL AND HOPE FER THE BEST.
I... DIDN'T REALLY HAVE TIME TO THINK, ONCE I KNEW YOU WERE IN TROUBLE, I--

YOU FORFEITED THE RACE FOR ME?
OF COURSE I DID!
PROBABLY!
WHO CARES ABOUT SOME CRUMMY RACE WHEN THE LOVE OF YOUR LIFE IS IN DANGER!

I FEEL THE SAME WAY, HONEY.

WAIT--
--THAT'S WHERE I SAW THAT LOUSY BARON BEFORE!
AT THE SANTA MONICA CAMP--HE'S THE SO-AND-SO WHO SHOT ME OUT OF THE SKY!
ALLEZ!
CHERCHER L'ENDROIT!
WHILE I'VE GOT YA IN A GOOD MOOD, HONEY--
--THERE'S ONE LAST THING I GOTTA DO.
SOMEONE HAS TA WARN EVERYONE ABOUT THE NAZIS!
MEET ME AT THE FINISH LINE IN A COUPLE A' HOURS!
I'LL BE THERE, BUSTER.
BUT IF YOU AREN'T...!
HEY, WOULD I EVER LET YA DOWN?
THE SPEED FROM THIS FUEL IS INCREDIBLE!
I MAY JUST HAVE A SHOT OF CATCHING HIM!
FWOOSH
I'M COMIN' FOR YA, BARON.
THIS THING AIN'T FINISHED YET!

ART BY STEPHEN MOONEY

Wish
you were
Here!

ART BY GABRIEL RODRÍGUEZ COLORS BY LEN O'GRADY

SOMEWHERE ABOVE FRANCE. ALL HELL'S A-COMIN'.
"SO, PROFESSOR NKOSI, ANY COMMENT AS TO WHERE YOUR EXPERIMENTAL PLANE MIGHT BE?
"NOT TO MENTION ITS PILOT, CLIFF SECORD?
"HE STILL HASN'T REACHED THE LATEST CHECKPOINT, WHEREAS RACE LEADERS, THE IRON BARON AND DEBBIE SEVILLE, PASSED THAT POINT OVER 30 MINUTES AGO!
"IS SECORD REALLY THAT FAR BEHIND, OR IS THIS MERELY PART OF THE PLAN YOU REFERRED TO IN YOUR LONDON PRESS CONFERENCE?
"IS THIS WHERE THE WORLD LEARNS OF THE TRUE GENIUS OF DELTON NKOSI?"
"GENTLEMEN, GENTLEMEN. ALL WILL SOON BE CLEAR.
"A MAGICIAN DOES NOT REVEAL HIS METHODS BEFORE THE TRICK IS COMPLETE!"

"YOU SHALL HAVE TO TAKE ME AT MY WORD WHEN I TELL YOU THAT MY MAN SECORD IS NOT DONE YET!"
THERE THEY ARE!
DEBBIE'S RIGHT ON THE BARON'S TAIL!
HE'S CHANGIN' COURSE...?
WHAT THE HECK IS HE UP TO NOW?
THAT'S A PASSENGER PLANE--!
IF HE'S NOT CAREFUL, HE'LL--
THAT MADMAN JUST STALLED THAT DAKOTA'S ENGINES!
SPUT
BANG
DEB, YOU SEEIN' THIS?
--CLIFF?!
WHERE THE HELL HAVE YOU BEEN?!
NO TIME, JUST FOLLOW MY LEAD!
OH MY GOD.
YOU'RE HIM!

YOU'RE THE ROCKETEER!
WE GOTTA-- HMMPH!
WE GOTTA CORRECT THEIR PITCH!
MAYDAY, MAYDAY!
WE'RE STALLED, LOSING ALTITUDE--
--WAIT! WE'RE LEVELING OUT!
I'M WITH YA, FLYBOY!
CLIFF!
YOU'LL BREAK YOUR GODDAMN BACK!
JUST NEED TO...
...GIVE THEM A CHANCE...

WE DID IT--
--THEY'RE REGAINING CONTROL!

TALK TA ME, FLYBOY--
--ARE YOU ALL RIGHT?
THE FORCE OF THAT THING...

I'M OKAY, I THINK.
GONNA BE SORE IN THE MORNIN'...

I DON'T BELIEVE IT...
...YOU'RE REALLY HIM.
YEAH.
NOW--
--LET'S CATCH THAT NAZI BASTARD!

TEAM NKOSI
I DON'T CARE WHERE YOU HAVE TO SEARCH, FIND MY BLOODY PLANE!
WHEN I GET MY HANDS AROUND SECORD'S THROAT HE'LL WISH HE'D NEVER LEARNED TO FLY!

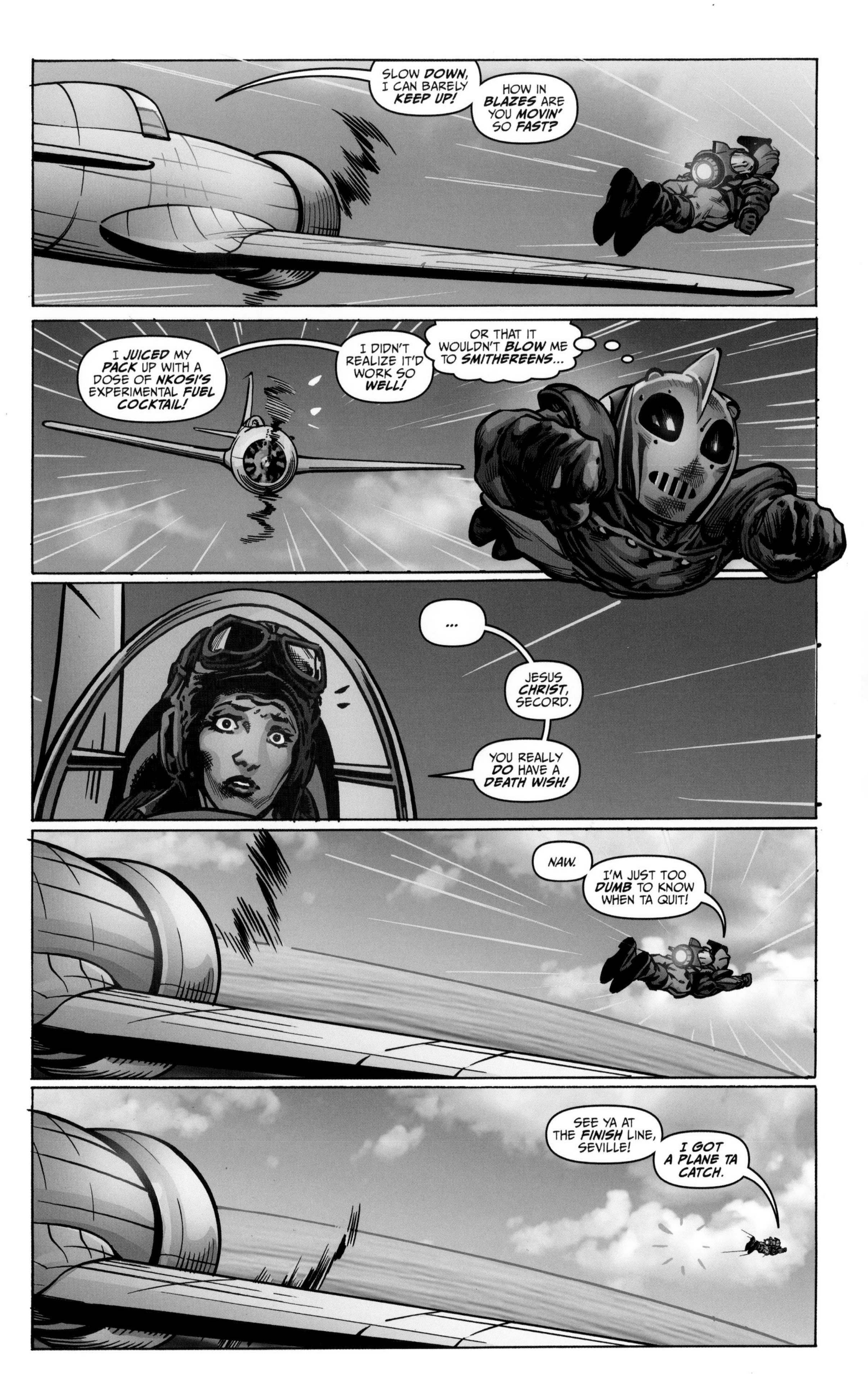
SLOW DOWN, I CAN BARELY KEEP UP!
HOW IN BLAZES ARE YOU MOVIN' SO FAST?
I JUICED MY PACK UP WITH A DOSE OF NKOSI'S EXPERIMENTAL FUEL COCKTAIL!
I DIDN'T REALIZE IT'D WORK SO WELL!
OR THAT IT WOULDN'T BLOW ME TO SMITHEREENS...
...
JESUS CHRIST, SECORD.
YOU REALLY DO HAVE A DEATH WISH!
NAW.
I'M JUST TOO DUMB TO KNOW WHEN TA QUIT!
SEE YA AT THE FINISH LINE, SEVILLE!
I GOT A PLANE TA CATCH.

THE FINAL OBSTACLE HAS BEEN ACCOUNTED FOR.
INFORM THE FÜHRER--

--VAS?

HI!
WHAT?
THE ROCKETEER?!

WHOA!
RATATAT
RATATATAT

RATATATATAT
ALLEY-OOP!
KA-PWANG
BLAM
AAARGGGH!
BLAM
CURSED AMERIKANER!
SO LONG, BARON--
--YER GROUNDED, PAL.
FWA-BOOM

FINISH
P-KOOOOM
OH MY GOD!
THE GERMAN PLANE HAS EXPLODED!

I CAN'T BELIEVE WHAT I'M SEEING!
HEY, BARON!
SORRY I CAN'T STOP TA CHAT, BUT I'VE GOT A RACE TO--
NNRRAAAGH!
KOFF
SPUTTER

UH-OH...
SOMETHIN'S SCREWY WITH THE ROCKET!
IT'S JERKIN' AROUND SOMETHIN' FIERCE!
WHRRR

GOTTA LAND AND GET IT OFF--
POP

RAAARGH!
ANOTHER EXPLOSION?!
FOOM
WHAT THE--?

BUT WAIT!
IS THAT...?
DEBBIE SEVILLE HAS WON THE INAUGURAL GREAT RACE!
HNNNHH
DID I... WIN?
WIN?
KLONG
OOOFF!
SCHWEINHUND...
...YOU ARE ABOUT TO LOSE...
...EVERYTHING!

HOOOFF
I WILL KILL YOU, AS I SHOULD HAVE DONE IN CALIFORNIA!
THUNG
MY BEAUTIFUL KOMET...
I SHALL DESTROY YOU, AS YOU DESTROYED IT!
WAIT... IT CANNOT BE!
IS THAT... SECORD?!
ONCE AGAIN I AM IMPRESSED!
I DID NOT THINK YOU CAPABLE OF SUCH CHICANERY!
NOW THAT I KNOW WHO YOU ARE, I WILL FIND YOUR WOMAN!
I WILL SHOW BETTY WHAT A TRUE MAN CAN DO!

Y-YOU...
WHAT WAS THAT, SECORD?
YOU WILL HAVE TO SPEAK UP!
YOU...
WHOK
UGH!
...WILL...
SLAMM
ARGHH
...NOT!
KRUGH
RARGH
NEVER!
*
KLONG
I'LL...
HUFF
I'LL...

-HUFF-
OH NO...
...THIS LOUSY THING.
WEE-OOO WEE-OOO
SO.
YOU FINALLY FINISHED THE RACE.
YOU HAVE COST ME EVERYTHING, SECORD.
OR, SHOULD I SAY, ROCKETEER?!
I RECOGNIZE THE AROMA, YOU SEE?
CLEVER, I MUST ADMIT, USING MY OWN FUEL BLEND TO PROPEL YOUR PACK.
BUT ALSO STUPID AND UTTERLY RECKLESS.
DO YOU REALLY BEAR SUCH DISDAIN FOR YOUR OWN SORRY EXISTENCE?
NO MATTER--
--AFTER ALL, I KNOW A GOOD DEAL WHEN I SEE ONE.
YOU HAVE STOLEN MY TECHNOLOGY. ALLOW ME TO RETURN THE FAVOR!

WHAMM
HRNNN!
GOD, HE TALKS A LOT.
HEY, FLYBOY.
NICE OUTFIT.

DETAIN THEM BOTH!
YOU... YOU'RE WITH THEM?!
SOMETIMES.
MY LIFE IS... COMPLICATED.
SOMETHING I'M SURE YOU CAN APPRECIATE.
YOU HAVEN'T JUST DEPRIVED ME OF MY PRIZE, SECORD!
YOU'VE COST THE WORLD A SAVIOR!
THE HEIGHTS I COULD HAVE REACHED WITH THAT MINERAL, THE PEOPLE MY TECHNOLOGY COULD HAVE HELPED!
GIVE IT A REST, PROF.
THE ONLY PERSON YOU WANNA HELP IS YERSELF.
FOR SOMEBODY WHO WANTS TA SAVE THE WORLD--
--YA SURE DON'T SEEM TA HAVE A PROBLEM WORKIN' WITH NAZIS.
I'D SAY THAT PUTS US ABOUT SQUARE.
OH, WE'RE A LONG WAY FROM SQUARE, YOU ARROGANT WHELP.
I'LL BE SEEING YOU AGAIN.

YEAH, YEAH...
...TELL IT TA THE JUDGE, LOUDMOUTH.

DELTON NKOSI, YOU ARE HEREBY PLACED UNDER ARREST FOR YOUR CRIMES AGAINST THE U.S. GOVERNMENT...
...AND COLLUDING WITH FOREIGN POWERS AGAINST U.S. INTERESTS. NOT TO MENTION TREASON.
...YER GOIN' AWAY FOR THE LONG HAUL, PALLY.

SO THOSE GOONS--
--HECK, I THOUGHT THEY WERE AFTER ME!
HOLD ON A SEC--DID YA PICK UP HIS AIRPLANE?

I DITCHED IT A WAYS BACK IN SOME OL' BARN.
I THINK THE NAZIS WERE AFTER IT!
YOU GOTTA--

PIPE DOWN, PAL.
GIMME A BREAK--

--YA WOULDN'T A' CAUGHT HIM WITHOUT ME!
DEBBIE, TELL THEM!
LET IT GO, CLIFF.
IT'S BEIN' TAKEN CARE OF.

JUST TELL ME WHAT YER GONNA DO WITH IT!
WE HAVE OUR TOP MEN WORKING ON IT.
WHO?!

C'MON, CLIFF.
LET'S SEE ABOUT GETTIN' YOU PATCHED UP.

SORRY ABOUT THE SMOKE AN' MIRRORS.
I FIGURE THE FACT I DON'T CONFISCATE WHAT'S LEFT OF THAT PACK MIGHT GO SOME WAYS IN ORDER OF AN APOLOGY?
AH, I AIN'T SORE, DEB.
I'M JUST GRATEFUL FOR THE SAVE.
AGAIN.

SO, YOU WERE REPORTIN' TO THE FEDS THE WHOLE TIME?
PRETTY MUCH.
WITH ME BEIN' IN THE RACE, IT WAS A SNAP TO MONITOR THE BARON. THEY KNEW HE WAS UP TO NO GOOD.
THE PLAN WAS FOR ME TA WIN THAT TROPHY AND KEEP IT OUTTA NKOSI'S MITTS.
THE BRASS HAD SUSPICIONS ABOUT HIM FOR A LONG TIME BUT NEEDED PROOF THAT HE WAS GONNA SELL TO THE KRAUTS.
IT WAS ONLY 'COS A' YOU THAT I WAS ABLE TA GET A WIRE ON THE ARROGANT BASTARD.

HEY, FLYBOY!
YOU NOT GONNA CONGRATULATE ME FOR WINNIN' THE RACE?
HA, SURE, JUST AS SOON AS YOU CONGRATULATE ME FOR WINNIN' OUR REMATCH!

CLIFF?!
HOW MANY TIMES ARE WE GOING TO DO THIS?
A 10

NO MORE, BETTS.
THE ROCKET IS DONE. I DON'T KNOW IF EVEN PEEVY CAN FIX IT THIS TIME.

GOOD.
I'M GLAD IT'S GONE.
MAYBE NOW WE CAN FINALLY MOVE ON WITH OUR LIVES.
ABSOLUTELY.
IN FACT--

OH, CLIFF!
REALLY?!
HUH?
OH, SORRY, BOOTLACE WAS UNTIED.
I WAS ABOUT TA SAY--
--IN FACT, LET'S GET STARTED RIGHT NOW!

I WANT YA TO KNOW SOMETHIN', BETTY.
IT'S FINALLY DAWNED ON ME--
--WHAT'S REALLY IMPORTANT.
AN' IT AIN'T NO DANGED ROCKET PACK, OR EVEN SAVIN' THE WORLD--
--IT'S YOU.
IT'S ALWAYS BEEN YOU.
SO WHADDYA SAY, BETTS?
THIS IS PARIS!
YOU'VE DREAMED OF MAKIN' IT HERE FER--
CLIFF.
STOP TALKING.
AND LET'S GO.
STEPHEN - FOR DAVE!

EPILOGUE 1.
WHEN WE EVENTUALLY GOT BOOTS ON THE GROUND AT THE RUSTIC CANYON SITE--
--THE FOREIGN AGENTS WERE LONG GONE.
WE SMOKED THESE RATS OUT, THANKS IN NO SMALL PART TO THE ASSISTANCE OF THIS ROCKETEER FELLOW.
BUT MARK MY WORDS, GENTLEMEN.
THERE ARE FAR GRAVER THREATS LOOMING ON THE HORIZON.
WE ARE AT THE BRINK OF WAR.
AND, VERY SOON, NOBODY WILL BE SAFE.

EPILOGUE 2.
BOY, OH BOY...
...THIS TIME HE BUSTED IT BUT GOOD.
WHAT A MESS.
MEBBE IT'S FER THE BEST, KID.
LOOKS LIKE WE MAY NEVER SEE THE ROCKETEER FLY AGAIN.

ART BY STEPHEN MOONEY

DAVE STEVENS AN ORAL HISTORY OF THE ROCKETEER

By *Kelvin Mao*

An oral history of Dave Stevens and *The Rocketeer*, conducted by Kelvin Mao, longtime friend of Dave's and director of the forthcoming documentary *Dave Stevens: Drawn to Perfection*. The interviews in the documentary were conducted by Mao and selected portions were culled together for this oral history.

In 1981, Dave Stevens was a professional illustrator living in Los Angeles. It had been six years since his first professional job as Russ Manning's assistant on various assignments, including the *Tarzan* and *Star Wars* newspaper comic strips. He was coming off a three-year stint working in animation at Hanna-Barbera, Filmation, and DePatie-Freleng and had just moved into a studio on La Brea Avenue with fellow artists Richard Hescox and William Stout.

Dave had also been a regular San Diego Comic-Con (later Comic-Con International) attendee since 1972 and been involved with its organization and growth—arranging art shows and contributing illustrations for attendee badges and souvenir program books and more. This included inking over the pencils of Jack Kirby, who had encouraged him from an early age.

Jackie Estrada (Longtime Comic-Con staffer and administrator of the Will Eisner Comic Industry Awards): "Dave was a member of the convention

Comic-Con Program book cover by Dave.

Comic-Con committee. We had two art shows, the professional and the amateur, so he was in charge of the amateur art show. I was the one that went to the artists and asked them to do illustrations and stuff for the progress reports and dealt with Dave as far as doing things like that."

Bob Chapman (Owner-operator of Graphitti Designs): "He was a big advocate of San Diego Comic-Con. So he always set up at San Diego, and this was before they had Artists' Alley and stuff. He always had his own booth there. And usually next to Bill Stout."

For the 1981 convention, Dave drew a beautiful Sheena, Queen of the Jungle pinup for the program book, which was also used for the first official Comic-Con T-shirt.

Bob Chapman: "In 1981, I approached Comic-Con and asked if I could do an event shirt. To produce them and to sell them. And was hoping to do a Batman shirt by a great Batman artist or something like that. They showed me the artwork they wanted on the shirt, and it was this Sheena with a monkey designed by this Dave Stevens guy who nobody had ever heard of."

This was one of Dave's first published good girl pinups, a genre he would become known for throughout his career. This image drew the attention of Steve and Bill Schanes, who had co-founded Pacific Comics, a local comics distributor. Capital City, a rival distributor, had just launched a modest publishing venture, debuting *Nexus*, a science fiction superhero comic by Mike Baron and Steve Rude. The Schanes brothers were looking to follow suit.

Jackie Estrada: "The editor at Pacific was Dave Scroggy, who had been the programming director at Comic-Con, and so Dave Stevens knew Scroggy. And of course, the Schanes brothers were the owners of Pacific Comics. They had been dealers at Comic-Con starting from the very first, I think, show in 1970. First they were kind of dealers out of their house, then a store, then they became a publisher, and then a distributor. So they went through all the phases."

To make a big splash, the first title they released was *Captain Victory and the Galactic Rangers* by comics legend Jack Kirby. Kirby had left comics in 1978 to focus on animation work, so to entice him back, Pacific made a deal to purchase only the publishing rights, allowing

Dave Stevens posing with a Rocketeer helmet.

Kirby to retain ownership and copyrights. This was something unheard of at the time. Pacific's next title was Mike Grell's *Starslayer*.

David Scroggy (Former comics editor and executive): "My place on the Comic-Con committee won me a real job with Pacific Comics, who, in those days, was a comics retailer in San Diego and needed a manager. When they became a distributor and closed down their retail stores, my title changed to editorial director. So I was focused on the publications."

Mark Evanier (Comics writer and historian): "Pacific Comics went to Dave and said, 'You want to do something?' Pacific was revolutionary at the time because there was really no intelligent place where you could create a comic and not lose total ownership of it immediately. Steve Schanes and Bill Schanes had formed a company to lure people away from the talent pool that DC and Marvel generally tapped into, made this very nice

Photo of ***Commander Cody****, one of Dave's key influences for* ***The Rocketeer****.*

creator-ownership deal, and I think Dave was one of the first people they approached."

David Scroggy: "Pretty much everybody who ever met Dave in his early days recognized his talent. It was obvious, from his high school teachers to college, to the conventions, to the professionals Dave met at the conventions. So it didn't take a rocket scientist to figure out this kid had the right stuff, that he was a special talent."

Mark Evanier: "Dave, having grown up around comic people like Kirby and Siegel and Shuster and was quite well aware of what it did to you to create something and then lose ownership to it. And now he had this opportunity. Mike Grell was doing this *Starslayer* book and didn't have time to do, like, a six- or seven-page chunk in the back, and they gave it to Dave. And that's where *The Rocketeer* was born."

After San Diego Comic-Con, Dave returned to Los Angeles and began noodling on a character design. He took inspiration from his childhood love of Republic Pictures serial films to create a new character that suited his sensibilities.

Richard Hescox (Fantasy artist and former studio mate of Stevens'): "Dave seemed to have been born in the 1920s and grew up in the 1930s and '40s, and somehow got teleported to our time. It was his love of those old serials—both of us from our childhood days, we used to watch them on early TV. And they were just inspirational to an imaginative kid."

William Stout (Fantasy artist and former studio mate of Stevens'): "Dave was at my studio when he created *The Rocketeer*. Initially, Scroggy got him to come into Pacific and Dave brought along a picture of *Commando Cody* that he had drawn, the Rocketman from the serials. And Dave said, 'This is a comic book I want to do.'"

David Scroggy: "We were all so young and clueless that Dave thought it was in the public domain, but none of us were sure. We were all too green and unsophisticated to know anything about licensing."

William Stout: "So Dave said, 'You know what? Well, let me take this back, let me come up with something similar, but I'll change enough so that it's really my own.' And what that ended up being was *The Rocketeer*."

Dave had originally envisioned the character of Cliff Secord to be a red-haired, freckle-faced guy in the vein of actor Sterling Holloway.

Mark Evanier: "Dave was drawing *The Rocketeer* all the time, designing the character. The early sketches with the helmet off didn't look that much like Dave. But with every proceeding sketch, he looked a little more like Dave."

Glen Murakami (Animator): "The great thing about *The Rocketeer* was, it wasn't all the obvious stuff. It wasn't, 'He's fighting Nazis, and he's Captain America.' Cliff was a reluctant hero. He was bratty and selfish and then ended up being a

Doug Wildey...

good person in spite of himself. And I think that's the aspect of *The Rocketeer* that I really liked. And I don't think anyone's matched it."

Scott Shaw (Animator and cartoonist): "It also should be noted that it was never a secret that the Peevy character was based on Doug Wildey."

Geofrey Darrow (Comic artist and film designer): "I met Doug Wildey through Dave Stevens and knew his work from when I was a kid watching *Jonny Quest*. Dave would talk about how cantankerous he could be."

Mark Evanier: "Doug had the office next door to mine in that corner of the Hanna-Barbera building. He was an amazing, colorful gentleman who had produced the *Jonny Quest* TV show, created it, and had had a lot of comic book credits. He was also a very charismatic, funny guy who was fun to be around and became a father figure to a lot of the young artists."

Scott Shaw: "Dave came to Hanna-Barbera in 1978 to work on the *Godzilla* show, which Doug Wildey was producing. He and Doug were personality-wise kind of polar opposites, but they

...and Doug Wildey.

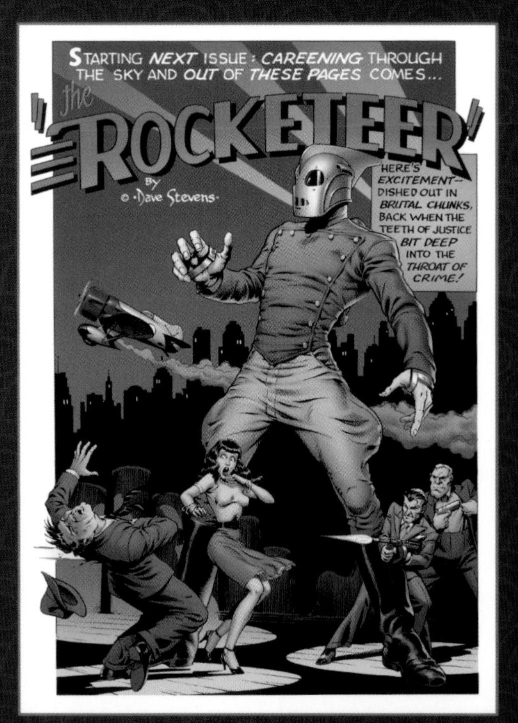

The first appearance of ***The Rocketeer****, the back cover ad in* ***Starslayer*** *#1.*

got along so well. And the thing people noticed was Dave was just as meticulous doing layouts as any other drawings that he did. The problem was, layouts were just a guide used for the animators. Those drawings never wound up in the cartoon, and Dave would maybe do one or two a day and everybody else was doing six or seven. But Dave never got hassled about his slow turnaround because he was Doug's favorite young protégé."

Bob Schreck (Comic editor): "He adored Dave, and they both just were super connected the minute they met. That's why Doug fought for him. But, yeah, he was Peevy. He was this wise guy. He's always had an answer, and Dave took it because he knew this guy was better than he was."

Mark Evanier: "Dave and Doug bonded, and the next thing we knew, Doug was in *The Rocketeer*."

Dave drew and submitted an illustration to Pacific Comics that the Schanes brothers approved and published as the first *Rocketeer* advertisement. It appeared in the back of *Starslayer* #1 in February 1982.

Geofrey Darrow: "I saw the ad for it in Pacific Comics. I think it was in the back of that Mike Grell comic—*Starslayer?* I was like, 'Wow! I'd buy that comic for like the six pages of beauty they had in the back.'"

Glen Murakami: "In 1982, a friend of mine called me and described a new comic book that had just come out. 'It's not Marvel or DC. It's this different company.' I'm like, 'What are you talking about? There's no such thing.' *Starslayer* #1 had the back cover with *The Rocketeer* ad, and that's the first time I saw the *Rocketeer*. That also primed me for comics that were different from mainstream. The thing about Dave Stevens is, he drew better than the Marvel and DC artists. That was another thing that was really intriguing to me."

Richard Hescox: "He had to come up with an image, an advertising piece of artwork. So he threw in all the elements he wanted—some tuxedo-clad gangsters, of course Bettie Page, a giant figure of the Rocketeer, and, like, a big city or New York in the background. Now, some of that stuff didn't wind up being in *The Rocketeer*, but he just created it with all the stuff he loved, threw it in there, and they printed it in Pacific Comic saying, 'Coming soon.'"

There was no stress for Dave going into the project because he was only committed to drawing two six-page chapters. The whole concept came very spur of the moment, and he tackled the story without long-range plans or concern for things like continuity or ongoing villains. Prior to this, the only comic story Dave had written was *Aurora,* for the Sanrio Company in 1977. His approach to what would become *The Rocketeer* was to imagine the perfect imagery that would visually jump off the newsstand and compel him to buy a comic book.

Geofrey Darrow: "*The Rocketeer* is very autobiographical. When I would read it, I'd go, 'This is sort of Dave minus the rocket pack. This is Dave Stevens' life, and he put the people and the things he liked into it.'"

Brinke Stevens (Actress and Stevens' ex-wife): "*The Rocketeer*, even though it was about a rocket pack, was really the story of us. I was modeling for Betty, and Dave was clearly Cliff. Marco of Hollywood expressed Dave's jealousy over my modeling for Ken Marcus and things like that. So *The Rocketeer* was very personal to me."

Bob Schreck: "Every storyteller has got to know their subject really well. They've got to love it and consume it and love it again, and watch everything you can and see everything you can about that time period. And, clearly, it was in his veins."

Glen Murakami: "Dave incorporated cultural things into his artwork. He took everything that he liked and shoved it into one thing. The cars, the airplanes, the movie serial aspect—it just had a lot of style and was very California. I had never seen that before, but I think that taught me that you can put what you love all into one work."

Dave wanted to craft a story that harkened back to those Republic serials except without the Martians, monsters, or flying through outer space. Something more grounded in reality with just the single gadget of the rocket pack thrown in so he could play with how the characters responded and dealt with it. He would use this project to pay homage to many of the artists and artistic movements that influenced him growing up.

Jim Silke (Pinup artist): "*The Rocketeer* is an expression of his aesthetic, and there's a lot of passion in that. It's a vision that combines a lot of things—his love of yesterday, of the serial movies, not just the major features but what RKO and Republic did in the ordinary run-of-the-mill Saturday-afternoon matinee kind of things. *Jungle Girls, Masked Villains, Rocketman*—obviously that's the influences of *The Rocketeer*. And the architectural artifacts of Los Angeles, the bulldogs—that all goes together to form an aesthetic that is so unique from a guy his age."

Dave at work in his shared La Brea studio.

Adam Hughes (Comic book and pinup artist): "His approach really opened up for me that whole world of old Hollywood, the golden age of Hollywood, and '30s art deco. I don't think I would have known about them if it wasn't through his work."

Dave Stevens with the Rocketeer bronze statue.

Jim Silke: "Here he's doing something new that he'd never done before. He'd done a comic, I guess—*Aurora*—and so forth. He worked with Russ Manning. He knew that aspect of it, but this was something... This was a dream, *Rocketeer,* all of a sudden coming."

William Wray (Comic book artist): "Dave had all the Frazetta *Buck Rogers* covers up, as a reference point, and he was working on *Rocketeer,* and he starts pulling it all down. We're like, 'Dave, I think we all know you and the Frazetta love. Relax, I do the exact same thing.'"

Mark Evanier: "Dave was influenced by the old illustrators, like Leyendecker and people like that. I think there were parts of Dave that wished he'd been drawing in the 1930s. He was influenced on a personal level or an artistic level by Jack Kirby, Alex Toth, Wally Wood—a lot—Al Williamson, Jim Steranko, Mike Sekowsky. He loved Mike Sekowsky's work."

William Stout: "Dave was a phenomenal brush inker. Brush inking is becoming a lost art. There were just such a small handful of guys who were really good with inking with a brush. I named them the Lost Brushman of the Kalahari. That was Frank Frazetta, Dave Stevens, Mark Schultz, and it was just guys who fell in love with inking with a brush."

Adam Hughes: "What are the ingredients of success? It's a random cocktail, and it's the artist, it's the creator, it's the characters, it's the setting, it's how it's presented, it's the time that it's unleashed on the world. And I think that's what *The Rocketeer* benefited from—that it hit all the right things at the right time for that particular cocktail."

Dave wanted to draw an adventure strip about a hero with flaws. One without superpowers, who could be hurt. And without resorting to graphic depictions of violence. Those first two installments weighed in at 11 pages capped off by a cliffhanger—Dave's own little serial on paper. And in his mind, a quick throwaway project just for fun. After the first chapter in *Starslayer* #2 came out in April 1982, one of the first fan letters Pacific Comics Presents received came from Michael Kaluta, who met Dave while both were being tapped to do *Star Wars* art.

Michael Kaluta (Fantasy and comic artist): "Come 1977, I was on my way to the San Diego Comic-Con. I walked into the middle of the El Cortez, and there were all these guys, pretty much my age, all talking about *Star Wars* because it had just come out. Dave was one of these guys. And from that point on, it was as if we had grown up together or something. What impressed me when *The Rocketeer* started coming out—Dave had captured his whole world. It was like something that I had grown up with but didn't remember until I saw the pages. So fully realized."

Dave Stevens, Richard Hescox, and William Stout.

Richard Hescox: "When it came down to actually doing the book, he had to sit down and write an actual story. And so things changed from his original image, but the Rocketeer himself didn't. It was still the same uniform, same helmet. When Dave was working on *The Rocketeer*, he would lay out his pages first in small thumbnails, then later on big tracing paper, and finally he'd trace it down and do the final inking. I remember him agonizing about the helmet because to make it work and have a human head inside, it would look cartoonishly big. He had to basically live with the idea that the helmet would actually be the character's head, size-wise. But the main thing is, aesthetically, it looked good. It read right; it was graceful. So he just swallowed the bullet because he was a fanatic for accuracy and had to not make the head the correct size."

Bob Chapman: "Dave doing strip work was draining. He did it thinking, 'Okay, I got this out of my life.' Not that it would go any further. Then, all of a sudden, people started writing letters. All of a sudden, he gets a fan letter from Michael Kaluta that says, 'Oh, Dave, *The Rocketeer* is great.' Shit like that. And it was pretty damn incredible."

Fan mail really poured in after the second chapter in *Starslayer* #3 was released in June 1982.

David Scroggy: "*The Rocketeer*, it took off like the Rocketeer. It was an immediate success."

Mark Evanier: "I can't recall too many strips that ever appeared and became star features instantly… Some time during the second or third page of that comic, the whole industry fell in love with it."

And it was no coincidence because Dave had introduced another object of his admiration in chapter 2, and that was Bettie Page, the '50s pinup queen. She was Dave's perfect embodiment of the female figure, and he had been drawing her for years.

Jim Silke: "In the second issue, I think it was *Starslayer* #3, a month later, there was Bettie Page. I've been drawing Bettie Page since 1951, simply because she was great to draw. And here's this young pup who came along, put her in a comic book."

Richard Hescox: "Early on in the studio, Dave introduced me to what he termed the best pinup model of all time. He was very enamored of her work and her figure. And he had a large collection of original photographs done way back when of her."

Mark Evanier: "And it was just a natural evolution that the two interests should merge, because if the character was Dave Stevens, the ideal woman was Bettie Page."

Jim Silke: "Dave said that when Secord needed a girlfriend, there was Bettie. And so he went with it. He'd been looking at her since he was 10 or 12 years old and even had some of the films, as I recall."

William Stout: "I had an old 16-millimeter projector at the studio, and at night, Dave would bring his Bettie films in, and we'd just project them on the wall. And for me, it was like, 'Who is this woman? And god, she's got the brightest smile and the most wholesome attitude I've ever seen for a gal who did burlesque and stuff.' I think Dave was well into Bettie Page before he ever moved into the studio."

Jaime Hernandez (Comic book creator): "When Dave put Bettie in his comics, I remember going, 'Oh, that's the lady from those old pinup photos. I didn't know who that was, the one with the bangs.' And that was the first time she had a name for me. 'Oh, Bettie Page. Okay, now I know who this is.' Dave was always getting photos from collectors, and he'd go, 'Look at these. Look at these!'"

Brinke Stevens: "I really had no idea who Bettie Page was. Then Dave showed me some 1950s pinup magazines that she was in, and I got it. I saw that she had a playful but sultry girl-next-door kind of quality. And Dave pretty much single-handedly brought her back into the public eye."

Pacific Comics had a hit on their hands with *The Rocketeer*, and Steve Schanes called Dave

Dave receiving his Russ Manning Most Promising Newcomer Award from Milton Caniff at San Diego Comic-Con in 1982. Sergio Aragones is in the background.

to give him the news and ask him to draw a monthly title. Dave wasn't prepared to work on the story at that pace for even one more chapter, but Pacific realized that Dave had delivered a flagship character and a potential moneymaker.

William Wray: "Dave's early *Rocketeer* work was easier for him. I don't think he had any preconceived notions. He didn't know that many people yet either. I don't even think he had the concept of getting other people to draw for him."

Michael Kaluta: "Talking with him about his work, he felt that he didn't really deserve that kind of praise. One of the things he really came down on himself about was the page layout. He said, 'I don't, I can't, I can't lay the page out. You know, it's just, it doesn't go anywhere.' And my response was, 'Whatever it is that you do, you do it excellently. It's got, it smells like old stuff. It smells authentic. The eye reads it, and it gets rewarded at every panel because of the way you do it.'"

At 1982's SDCC, due in large part to his *Rocketeer* work, Dave was awarded the first annual Russ Manning Promising Newcomer Award.

Jackie Estrada: "After Russ died, it was created in his memory to recognize the promising newcomers in the field. The ceremony was in the basement of the Hotel San Diego, and Ruth Clampett was on hand to give out the award. And the very first award did go to Dave Stevens, who had been Russ' assistant. Dave was just really touched, and everybody was all teared up."

Bob Chapman: "Seeing him win the award, especially with Russ Manning being his mentor and somebody he worked with, and somebody who he talked about, was emotional."

*Front cover of **Pacific Presents** #1.*
*The bottom half is Steve Ditko's **The Missing Man**.*

David Scroggy: "We couldn't imagine anyone else winning. I have no idea how many people participated in the voting, but I wouldn't be surprised to hear it was unanimous. So it was with a kind of pride that we saw him accept it."

Despite some apprehension, Dave continued to draw a third *Rocketeer* chapter. But instead of being a backup, it would be a lead feature in an all-new series: *Pacific Presents*. The first issue featured a 12-page *The Rocketeer* installment—the longest one yet, paired with a Steve Ditko *Missing Man* backup story. *Pacific Presents* #1 was released in October 1982. That made it three *Rocketeer* comics in the same year, a pace that would never again be equaled.

William Stout: "Dave, despite his reputation, wasn't actually slow as an artist. I saw it when I watched him produce *The Rocketeer* out of my studio. When he was cooking, the pages would just fly off the table. He would really, really produce. But the thing is, Dave loved people. If he would get a phone call, that'd be an hour or two shot. So if he got three phone calls, the day was done, because he couldn't work and talk on the phone at the same time."

Jim Silke: "Dave would bitch and moan about everything and his deadlines, and then we'd go to lunch and talk for three hours."

Russ Heath (Comic book artist): "Dave, at one point, got behind on some of his earlier *Rocketeer* stuff and called me over to help. The best part of any artist is his unique personality, and you can't get that from someone else. And I thought, that rarely works out. But I ran over and so on. We ended up going to one of those terrible delicatessens he always talked about and had dinner. So I can only imagine Dave must've gotten further behind because I 'helped' him."

Bob Chapman: "When Dave was motivated to draw, he drew like a son of a bitch. He could produce, but Dave wasn't disciplined. He was very emotional and talented, and maybe disciplined in how he worked with a brush and the magic he could do there, but disciplined mentally, no. That's not a word that should be thrown in this mix here. And I say that with all love and respect."

Dave had written the third chapter without planning out any long-term direction for the character. With success came expectations from both fans and his fellow artists. Dave's sense of professional integrity compelled him to try to make his stories better and better, to top himself each time. But he struggled to handle drawing the strip alone. Pacific Comics was a small operation with no staff to help, and most of Dave's friends were busy with their own projects.

Jaime Hernandez: "Dave was usually satisfied when it was a quick job. He seemed happier with *He-Man* drawings than *Rocketeer* comics, I think, because he didn't have to take it personally. It's the thing Dave struggled most with. One day he told me, 'I've got to finish this next *Rocketeer* book.' He goes, 'But I'm not a cartoonist. I got talked into this.' I was like, 'Okay, I half believe you.'"

Michael Kaluta: "His astoundment went to the fact that he had to produce more. I'm sure that he debated with himself over all sorts of story plot ideas as he was trying to cobble them together. But then when he got into it, there was so much more there."

David Scroggy: "With *The Rocketeer*, being the editor in the sense of wrangling the work was an exercise in frustration, as every other editor since then can tell you. I did try to get into his art process enough to help him be more confident in his decisions. A lot of his revisions were really not improvements but simply lateral moves. It wasn't better, just a little different. And so I tried to help grow his confidence, but I would say that I was a failure."

Brinke Stevens: "Dave had such a natural talent. He seemed to have a clear idea inside his head, what he wanted. He would totally visualize it, do a rough little sketch. Then I would pose. He would take lots and lots of photos. The poses were pretty precise. And then he would do more sketches and refine his art. It was a lengthy process."

John Koukoutsakis (Longtime friend of Stevens' and comics retailer): "Lengthy. Oh my god. He would noodle out something on a page and go, 'Wow, that's pretty good. I want the pose to look like that.' He'd do it in, like, ten minutes. Six months later, it's like, 'I'm still inking the eyebrow, and I'm erasing it every other day and re-inking it.' So, yeah, his process was very lengthy."

Jaime Hernandez: "I remember being at Dave's house when he and Hescox were working on a paperback cover. They went out in the backyard and Dave did poses for Hescox while he shot, and then Dave would take photos of him. Dave would even put on his Rocketeer outfit. They just helped each other out like that."

Richard Hescox: "Dave, me, and Bill Stout would pose for each other's illustrations. We were all together in a room. If you needed a model or to figure out how a pose should look, there was somebody usually right there. And you say, 'Could you hold your hand up like this, put this helmet on, and pretend to strangle me or something?' We were trying to be frugal, and professional models were expensive. Dave appeared in 20 or 30 of my book covers, and I appeared in *The Rocketeer* and other illustrations that he and Stout did."

From the third chapter on, Dave warned Pacific Comics repeatedly that it was going to take a long time for each new chapter. He was doing the writing, penciling, inking, and coloring of each installment by himself.

David Scroggy: "Part of the frustration we had with Dave's speed was because the market was clamoring for more. We had intended it as a backup feature, whereas *The Rocketeer* was obviously worthy of its own book and driving the sales of this comic, even though it was only, what, six pages a go."

Adam Hughes: "The area where Dave and I are alike is we're both apocalyptically slow. We'd rather do it right than do it quick."

Dave and Jaime Hernandez.

Richard Hescox: "Working in comic books by the traditional system, he was not going to make a lot of money. He was just not fast enough and didn't want to be fast enough. He wouldn't have been happy doing things faster when he finally had his own character of the Rocketeer."

David Scroggy: "So trying to rearrange the priorities of that to turn *The Rocketeer* into the lead was challenging because there wasn't enough *Rocketeer* to support an ongoing dated periodical, let alone monthly. A Pacific lead feature was probably at least 20 pages back in those days. So that was what was expected of a lead feature in a comic book. And for Dave to maintain anything remotely approaching that schedule was just impossible. But the demand for it was overwhelming, so we did the best we could to try to think of other kinds of stuff. But how popular was *The Rocketeer*? It started off as popular as you could imagine and grew from there."

In addition to the comic, Dave had more lucrative advertising and film production work he needed to take on to pay the bills. At

the end of the day, Dave was receiving around $150 per page for everything. But he continued on because he loved comics his whole life and always wanted to draw his own characters. The book required extensive research as well. If Dave made a mistake with an aircraft or period detail, fans would let him know through letters or in person at conventions. Their investment in the series was a big factor in his continuing to do it.

Mark Evanier: "*The Rocketeer* is a strip with which the creator is so intimately involved with every pose and every person in it, and every background and every part of it, nothing was ad-libbed. Dave had to know exactly what was going on in every corner of every panel."

Geofrey Darrow: "Dave used a lot of archival photos of restaurants and airplanes, and he'd go to airplane shows sometimes. But he also had bought a Mauser, an actual pistol, that he could draw from."

Bruce Timm (Animator on *Batman: The Animated Series* and many more): "One of the things I love about *The Rocketeer* stuff, especially those first couple stories, is kind of how loose and lumpy it was, because clearly, he didn't really care that much about it. The Schanes brothers said, 'Yeah, 12 pages, whatever it is, I don't care. We got half a book to fill in the back, whatever you want.' And so he just kind of did it as a lark, but then once he started getting attention for it, it was like, 'Oh no, now I got to really step up my game. Everything's got to be… I have to make this as good as people think it is.'"

Glen Murakami: "At one point, everyone wanted to ink like Dave. Everyone tried to ink like Dave, but no one was good enough to pull it off. No one could figure it out. And *The Rocketeer* took so long to come out, so we also knew that was part of it. It must not be easy if it takes that long to produce."

But Dave also recognized his art was improving with each chapter. He saw a real difference from chapter one to chapter three, both stylistically and dynamically, and he was enjoying the challenge of seeing how far he could go.

William Stout: "When the pages began to emerge, I was astounded. The quality of the writing, the quality of the penciling and inking and design was just jaw-dropping. It was really the best thing being done in comics back then. And it was a joy for me to come into the studio each day and see what Dave had done the previous evening."

David Scroggy: "I really had an interesting catbird seat to see the numerous revisions he would go through, all the partially finished things and pages Dave ripped up, the little bits Dave would extend from the borders. *Pacific Presents* #5…it's kind of a triptych cover with Betty in the bottom right corner where you just get her bustline, but Dave continued beyond the borders. That kind of thing."

Mark Evanier: "Everything was very deliberate and planned. Sometimes he would do a dozen sketches before he was satisfied with the position of the hand. And it got more and more pronounced as he developed a reputation and felt he had to live up to it. I think there were times he would have been happier doing work under a pseudonym."

Bob Schreck: "He was meticulous and a perfectionist. You would look at the same page that he just finished and go, 'Oh my god, this is gorgeous.' He's like, 'Eh.' He really thought about everything, every line, every mood. He had color in his brain. He knew exactly where he was going before he went there. There's the famous story about him not being able to finish that bulldog's leg when he was in the studio."

William Stout: "I remember he had almost finished an entire *Rocketeer* story, and there's one panel left that had a bulldog, and that bulldog was completely inked except for one leg. And that sat on his desk for, god, it seemed like weeks, because he wanted to get just the right reference to be able to do that leg as properly as possible, and it was just driving me nuts. It was like, 'Dave, just ink it. Just ink it. You'll be done with the book.'"

Richard Hescox: "It was an absolutely finished page except for one dog's paw. He must have gone back to that paw six, seven, eight, I don't know how many times, and redrew it because he wasn't happy with it. All he had to do was put a couple of lines of ink on and be paid, but he was not going to let it go until he was sure that thatpaw was exactly how he wanted."

David Scroggy: "I felt very privileged watching this project. The meticulous construction of a page of *The Rocketeer,* times many pages of *The Rocketeer,* was a real memorable, educational process. A very frustrating one, but memorable."

The next issue was chapter four. It would not come out until the following year, but Dave's art reached new heights when *Pacific Presents* #2 was released in April 1983 with a *Rocketeer* chapter that clocked in at 13 pages.

Glen Murakami: "That shot of the Bulldog Café, with that golden sky, with the palm trees, that was an image I had never seen before. That was also a big deal. There's just something really lush about that comic book. Yeah, it was the pinup art, and the car culture, and the planes. It was real California; it was real West Coast in a way that no one represented before."

The infamous "paw" page!

Jackie Estrada: "He was obviously a terrific storyteller. He could get your eye on the page to move the way it should be moving and get the reaction out of the reader. And I'm fond of quoting Will Eisner, who said each page should tell a story. Each panel should tell a story. Each row of panels should tell a story. And I think Dave, even if he never heard Will say that, he incorporated that into his storytelling."

It was around this time in May of 1983 that Dave began working on a pitch for a *Rocketeer* film.

William Stout: "I think the first attempt that Dave made in getting a *Rocketeer* film off the ground came out of *Godzilla*."

Steve Miner (Film director): "I hired Bill Stout to do some concept art for a remake of *Godzilla*. Bill shared a studio with Dave and Richard Hescox on South La Brea Avenue in Los Angeles. I began spending a lot of time there and got to know Dave pretty well. It was a fun, productive atmosphere."

William Stout: "Steve saw Dave's comics, fell in love with them, and wanted to make *The Rocketeer* as a movie."

Steve Miner: "Everything about *The Rocketeer* screams movie—from its zeitgeist to a really hot femme fatale. It transports you, just like any good movie, into a world inhabited by flawed but extraordinary characters."

Since *The Rocketeer*'s debut, Pacific had expanded rapidly, taking on new titles. In 1984, they began to have problems with the distribution side of their business as competitors joined the expanding independent market.

David Scroggy: "Pacific Comics was a company that enjoyed great success by being the first truly

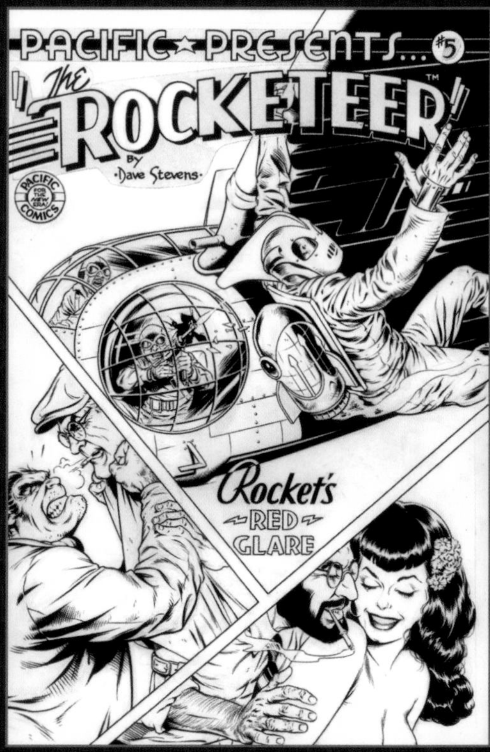

*Originally intended to be the cover of **Pacific Presents** #5, this was published as **Rocketeer Special Edition** #1.*

popular comic book company to give creators ownership and control of their own material. Prior to Pacific, the comics world had been very oppressive to creators. The classic stories are of Superman where their creators lost control, but it was the norm. With Jack Kirby, with all his Marvel characters, the stories are many and legion. But the Schanes brothers came along with a business model that awarded ownership of the characters, the underlying property, the original art, and paid it on a royalty basis. This was pretty unprecedented for a modern comic company, hence they were able to acquire talents like Jack Kirby, Neal Adams, and so on."

Eventually the glut of indie comics entering the market would lead to the collapse of Pacific Comics just as Dave was handing in the fifth and final 20-page chapter of the Rocketeer's first adventure, originally slated to run in *Pacific Presents* #5.

David Scroggy: "Well, these books were very popular, but for a variety of reasons, Pacific did not succeed. I describe it as being literally like a skyrocket. It went off in a great, brilliant arc into the sky and exploded. The years between 1981 or 1980, when we were really formulating the comics, were truly a skyrocket ride. And when the company went out of business, there wasn't a lot of warning."

Fortunately, Dave was soon contacted by another independent publisher—Eclipse Comics, which had been founded in 1977 by brothers Jan and Dean Mullaney. In November 1984, five months after Pacific folded, the fifth *Rocketeer* book was published as *The Rocketeer Special Edition* #1, which also included pinups by Dave's pals Doug Wildey, Michael Kaluta, William Stout, Al Williamson, Russ Heath, Bruce Jones, and others.

David Scroggy: "Dean Mullaney obviously saw the opportunity and reached out to Dave directly, and I'm sure was persuasive. He persuaded me, so why wouldn't he persuade Dave? And, at the time, Dean had funding for this adventure, so it was kind of an easy transition for Dave to go to Eclipse."

Jaime Hernandez: "People kept bugging him about making a *Rocketeer* collection out of those short chapters. Dave didn't think he could do it by himself and asked me to come and help."

With the help of Jaime Hernandez, Dave added extra pages and reformatted the original chapters in order to collect *The Rocketeer* story into one volume. Dave also wanted to recolor the early chapters, so he enlisted housemate Joe Chiodo, along with assistance from burgeoning young artists like Bruce Timm and Brent Anderson.

Bruce Timm: "Dave was getting ready to recolor the first three chapters of *The Rocketeer* for the collection in the painted style he had done in *Rocketeer Special Edition* to make it all match. He needed somebody cheap and fast. Mark Evanier and Dave were buddies from working at Hanna-Barbera. And even though I'd never done much coloring before, Evanier suggested me based on one comic that I'd done for him."

Jaime Hernandez: "I was invited to spend a couple of days at Dave's house to help him with new added pages to his first *Rocketeer* collection. I was instructed by Dave to pencil assorted figures and panels here and there, and to lay out and pencil one full page of Betty tied up fighting crooks in the backseat of a car. I remember when he started inking it, he called me over and said, 'Ya gotta give her that Betty cheek,' which was the cheek on her face, not her ass."

Bruce Timm: "At the time, Dave was living with Joe Chiodo in this tiny little house, I think built in the '20s, very old-fashioned looking. When I was coloring in the kitchen with Joe, I would sneak in occasionally and look over Dave's shoulder while he was drawing. I think he was still doing some of those last few insert pages that he had done with Jaime. And so he allowed me to watch him ink a page, and it was pretty fascinating. He was really slow. That's the thing about him—he was legendarily slow, but his line was so controlled. He was really, really, really slow and very careful."

Jaime Hernandez: "He called me 'Hurricane Hernandez' because he would say, 'Draw this,' and I would draw it, and then he'd go, 'Oh, you're done.' So he would try to give me something else to do."

Milton Caniff and Doug Wildey looking through ***The Rocketeer****, the collection of the first series.*

Bruce Timm: "Brent Anderson also colored some pages as well, but when I worked there, it was just me, Joe, and Dave. I had heard that Jaime was doing some penciling for him and maybe had already done it by the time I got there. And I think Russ Heath was supposed to help him out, but Dave basically said, 'Ah, he would just come over and drink beer and just shoot the shit.' So, I don't think Russ ever actually ended up doing any pages for him."

Bob Schreck: "I love Dave's coloring, and I think he used gray lines, but I loved his coloring eye. He really understood how to bring out certain aspects of the story and make your eye go to the right place. The thing I knew at the time, and flipped me out, was that he was using his own spit to make his colors better, and I was like, 'You're spitting?' And he'd go, 'Ah…sometimes you just gotta spit on the damn thing,' and take a Q-tip with his spit and kind of mottle the color. And it was like, 'Oh, that's gross.'"

Bruce Timm: "So Dave and whoever else first colored in this process figured out that the best way to color it was with watercolor markers—a brand called Stabilo, which I'm not sure they even make anymore. But it was a water-based ink, and you couldn't put the marker directly on the page. What you would do is, you'd have, like, a big box of Q-tips sitting right next to you, and you'd wet one with saliva in your own mouth, then push the tip of the marker onto the Q-tip, and use the Q-tip as your brush and kind of smear it onto the page. It sounds very imprecise, and you ended up using a lot of spit. But when I asked about this process, Joe Chiodo and Dave both said, 'Yeah, we tried lots of different solvents to work with the ink, and spit seemed to have the best viscosity.'"

The five-chapter *Rocketeer* collection was published the following year, in September 1985, as *The Rocketeer Graphic Album*, with an introduction by Harlan Ellison.

Bob Chapman: "Harlan Ellison was a very articulate and colorful person. He had a command of the English language that should be banned. He used words that—shit, they're not even in dictionaries. He had an energy and a vibrancy, but if you crossed him, he was worse than a pit bull. Harlan was a huge *Rocketeer* supporter for the nostalgic reasons, for the music reasons, everything about *Rocketeer* pushed Harlan's buttons, in a good way. Dave and Harlan had good chemistry. Their relationship with was always interesting to see."

Jessie Horsting (Writer of Cliff Secord history): "Harlan was a voracious comics reader and really appreciated good art. I imagine he sought Dave out to tell him what he thought of him. They got along really well, and Dave was a frequent visitor up at Harlan's. Harlan was one of the most decent, compassionate people I ever met. Which is not a description you hear from many people. He could be abrasive. He's outspoken. He can be rude and very difficult to get along with. But if you're in trouble or needed a hand, if he saw a situation where he could help, he would never hesitate."

William Stout: "One of my favorite pieces of Dave's was the cover he did of Sheena with the macaw. Boy, I wanted that piece really bad, but then it got stolen and was gone for a long time. Eventually, Dave found out who stole it and revealed that when Harlan Ellison was visiting our studio. Harlan's first response was, 'Hey, I've got a baseball bat. Let's go get it.'"

Jaime Hernandez: "I go, 'Yeah. Well, part of you wanted to do this comic.' But I can see how he was just so, like, 'I don't know how to make comic books. I'm too wound tight to do this,' kind of thing. He would always come to this point where he goes, 'Okay, I got three things I'm supposed to be working on. This is the month I'm going to wrap them all up,' and that's when he would ask people to help with *The Rocketeer* or whatever."

***The Rocketeer Graphic Album* won Dave both a Kirby Award for Best Graphic Album and an Inkpot Award at San Diego Comic-Con in 1986.**

Dave and Brinke Stevens posing for one of his studio mates' paintings. Stevens, Stout, and Hescox would often pose for one another's covers.

Jackie Estrada: "The Kirby Awards were founded by Fantagraphics. It was really the first comics industry awards that were a major big deal. They had Kirby's permission to use his name and a process for professionals in the industry to be involved, nominating and voting on the winners. It was an afternoon programming slot, maybe on Saturday, and Kirby was there to give the trophies to the winners. I have a photo of the 1986 Kirby Award winners, and Dave is there standing behind Kirby and Alan Moore."

Jackie Estrada: "With all the awards Comic-Con gives out, the Inkpots were the first. We started in 1974, I think. And those are ones that Comic-Con gives people for their contribution to whatever field of popular culture they're in."

David Scroggy: "This was another Shel Dorf brainchild for Comic-Con. He felt that they should have some award to honor the guests who came. They had an Inkpot Awards banquet on Saturday night of the convention."

One of the ten covers done by Dave for Eclipse, ***DNAgents*** *#24.*

The Rocketeer Graphic Album **went into two printings and was also released as a signed and numbered hardcover edition by Graphitti Designs in 1986. That version included a Cliff Secord biography on the inside flaps of the dust jacket.**

Jessie Horsting: "Dave's an artist who draws beautifully. That's how he thinks and tells stories. He was not a guy that sat down, had the story in his mind, and typed it out. He thought in sequences. Dave wanted to have a biography of Cliff Secord as part of the book. And he knew what Cliff looked like, where he was born, what day he was born on, how he met Peevy, how he met Betty. He knew everything about him but didn't know how to say it in six paragraphs or whatever the space was. That's where we were yin and yang. He would say, 'This is what I want to say about Cliff.' And I would go home and write it. He would make edits and give me his notes. And then we came up with exactly what he wanted, but he always knew exactly what he wanted."

Despite the success of *The Rocketeer* album, Dave had issues with Eclipse, who wanted the rights to publish future Rocketeer stories. Dave decided to leave Eclipse but agreed to do a run of ten spectacular covers for Eclipse titles from 1984 to 1986. Soon after, Dave moved *The Rocketeer* to Comico, a comics publisher based out of Norristown, Pennsylvania.

Bob Chapman: "There were some shenanigans going on at Eclipse, not with Dean specifically, but it was messy. People were not doing what they said they were going to do on their end, and it left a bad taste in Dave's mouth."

Bob Schreck: "The relationship at Eclipse did not last very long and didn't go well. Dave eventually gave us a call and said, 'Hey, Schreck, I'm ready to go. I'm getting out of here.' And because I knew Dave for all those years, and he knew my ex, Diana Schutz, as well, it was a no-brainer. The bottom line is, just be honest with people. And that's why he gave me a holler."

David Scroggy: "Eclipse was on the ropes at that point financially. Dave going on to Comico was... I guess Bob Schreck, probably Phil Lasorda, the then president of Comico, who maybe saw the opportunity. And Dave, because he could do what he wanted, be reasonably well paid, still own the Rocketeer, and have the same audience readership-wise he enjoyed previously, went with it."

In June of 1984, *The Rocketeer* was translated into French and appeared in issue #8/9 of a comics magazine called *Spécial USA*, which reprinted American and non-French comic stories. While planning out the next *Rocketeer* series for Comico in 1985, Dave met screenwriters Danny Bilson and Paul De Meo. They developed a new *Rocketeer* movie pitch and brought it to producer Lloyd Levin and

*Dave with the **Rocketeer** screenwriters Danny Bilson (left) and Paul De Meo (right).*

director William Dear, who was fresh off *Harry and the Hendersons.*

Jessie Horsting: "Dave had his eye on film. Especially after *Indiana Jones* came out, because it's the same era and sort of epic adventure. It just was a natural. And people were interested in it. I was working at MGM at the time, after the Graphitti Designs version. And I had just brought it to work, and one of the guys in development walked by my desk, saw the cover, and says, 'What is this? Are you trying to sell it?' And he said, 'Could I borrow this for a couple of hours?' And, apparently, he went to Alan Ladd Jr.'s office, who owned the studio at the time. People recognized right away what a property it could be, and I think Dave always planned for that."

Mark Evanier: "Dave seemed to always be talking to somebody about making a movie of *The Rocketeer,* and finally he connected with some people who were real filmmakers, real producers. It was not a 'let's raise the money, make it for a Roger Corman budget' film."

Danny Bilson (*The Rocketeer* co-screenwriter): "It all starts with Golden Apple Comics. Paul De Meo and I met in college and were working at Empire Pictures, Charlie Band's company. Our offices were on Fairfax, near Melrose, so we could walk to Golden Apple at lunchtime. Comics in the mid-eighties were really exciting, and we loved *The Rocketeer*. Paul and I loved old movies, so we were really, really attracted to it."

Jessie Horsting: "There're these young men who want to get out and work for a proper studio for a lot more money and better projects. That was where Danny and Paul were at that moment."

Danny Bilson: "And, for Paul and I, it was always art first. If the art wasn't good, no thanks. But *The Rocketeer* was like, holy cow, the art! So, we look into who's got the rights. Could we get the movie

Michael Kaluta's rendition of the Pitcairn autogyro.

rights to develop this? We were making movies at Empire, but we weren't any big deal. I think we had an agent, and they contacted Dave, I guess, or someone did. Steve Miner had the option on *The Rocketeer*, and it was just coming up for renewal."

Jessie Horsting: "So, it's like there's a buzz or an undercurrent that it was *The Rocketeer's* time. It was kind of in the air. A girl who used to work for Harlan Ellison had gotten a job with Empire Pictures and knew *The Rocketeer* from Harlan and me. Word got back to me that Danny and Paul wanted to meet Dave, and I facilitated that."

Danny Bilson: "Dave came into our office, and we pitched him what we wanted to do with *The Rocketeer*. This is probably around March or April of 1985. We were just back from making a movie called *Zone Troopers* in Italy, and the concept art was in the office. And it was all absolutely art deco. *Zone Troopers* was done as if it were made as a B movie in the '40s. I remember Dave sitting in our office when we said, 'We want to use the Creeper in *The Rocketeer*.' And it was like we had said some magic word."

Jessie Horsting: "They were very excited at the idea of *The Rocketeer* because they saw another *Raiders of the Lost Ark* in it."

Danny Bilson: "We thought Rondo Hatton, who was the Creeper, would be a great, menacing villain. And Dave was like, 'I always wanted to do the Creeper.' And that was the connection. It was the *Zone Troopers* art and Rondo Hatton. And what was interesting was we were all just kids who didn't have much money. But Dave gave us a free option on the movie. For the six years from that time until it became a movie, that was just a friend agreement."

As the wheels of Hollywood development slowly crept along, Comico published its first Dave Stevens cover, *Jonny Quest* #3 in August 1986. The first new Comico *Rocketeer* image was published the following year in April 1987 as the cover to *Comico Attractions* #6.

Bob Schreck: "And as an editor, all I want to do is tell them what they need to be told and then get out of their way. If you're going to hire Bernie Wrightson, then get out of his way. He's Bernie Wrightson, and the same thing with Dave. He knows what he's doing."

Shortly thereafter, Dave signed a movie deal with Disney, and *The Rocketeer* movie was officially announced in the August 1987.

Mark Evanier: "When they made the deal for *The Rocketeer* movie, Dave asked for some sort of guarantee that the Betty character would be Bettie. At this point, Bettie Page's whereabouts were unknown, and Disney said, 'No, we've got to change it just in case she surfaces and sues.'"

Jim Silke: "They were afraid of a lawsuit. And they wouldn't do Betty. Which cut the guts out of that character. Not that it had to be Bettie Page, but the things that she offered. It's not an ordinary girl. It's not that side of life."

Mark Evanier: "Dave was ready to blow the whole deal off because he thought Betty was as important an element of the property as the Rocketeer himself. His lawyer, Henry Holmes, and I went to lunch with Dave and talked him out of this. Henry said, 'No, you can't be a hundred-percent certain that Bettie is not going to surface someplace…'"

Danny Bilson: "There was a part of Dave that, I don't know. Sometimes I wondered if *The Rocketeer* was a vehicle for Bettie to be, to exist. That was really important to Dave."

Mark Evanier: "And then, sure enough, Bettie showed up a couple years later. I think Dave was ultimately happy he backed down on that, because otherwise somehow Disney would have had some sort of additional claim on her likeness, or there could've been a messy entanglement over that."

In July of 1988, *Rocketeer Adventure Magazine* #1 was released. It is the first chapter of a three-part story titled, *Cliff's New York Adventure* and introduces Cliff's friend Goose and the shadowy character Jonas. The issue also includes an article about the Pitcairn autogyros, as well as a *Galactic Girl Guides* backup story by Dave's friends Elaine Lee, Michael Kaluta, and Charles Vess.

Inspired by Rondo Hatton as the ***Creeper****, Dave incorporated his likeness into* ***Cliff's New York Adventure****, as well as later being used in the film.*

Bob Schreck: "One of my proudest achievements was working with Dave. We got really lucky. He was very, very into making these books happen. So we didn't have to put up with waiting for a bulldog's leg to be finally inked."

John Koukoutsakis: "I don't think he was close to any of his publishers. He was always mad at them because he never got paid on time, and they were always busting his chops about getting shit done. But Bob Schreck and Diana Schutz were his editors and took care of him. Diana did an interview with Dave and the *Telegraph Wire*, one of his first interviews, when she was working at Comico and comic stores in the Bay Area. Those two, he did love. But they weren't publishers. Those two, he did love, but they treated Dave like a normal person."

Bob Schreck: "I begged Dave to do a cover for our 1988 *Comico Christmas Special*, and I art directed it and said, 'Let's do this story. Just put these aliens on there and a little spaceship. It'll be great!' And he's like, 'Schreck, you don't know what you're doing. You're crazy. No one's going

BLAST OFF!

The time is 1938. The place is L.A. An ordinary guy and would-be stunt pilot named Cliff Secord comes into possession of a flying gizmo—developed by a scientist who's on the run from Nazis.

With that gizmo strapped to his back, and an ominous face mask/helmet to ensure his anonymity (and before you can say "super hero"), Cliff Secord becomes the crime-fighting . . . Rocketeer!

The unlikely hero, who first surfaced in Dave Stevens' "Rocketeer" comics (for Pacific Comics, in 1982), is headed for the screen.

William Dear, lately of "Harry and the Hendersons," will direct for producer Larry Gordon and the Disney studio. Creator Stevens is serving as creative consultant.

Currently supervising the film's script (by Danny Bilson and Paul DeMeo), Dear said: "I envision this as a big-screen comic book—with an edge. It won't have quite the nasty side of 'RoboCop' but it will be hard hitting."

The plot involves "nothing less than matters of consequence to the entire world." Of course, Secord's girlfriend, Betty, also will be involved. And as per the comics, Secord will hang out at the airfield.

As for a star: "Let's just say I'm willing to go to the mat to get an unknown who I happen to think is the one and only Cliff Secord."

—From Pat H. Broeske

From the ***Los Angeles Times****, August 1987, announcing the forthcoming* ***Rocketeer*** *film.*

to want this cover.' I'm like, 'But you're Dave Stevens. You increase sales just by doing a cover.' He fought me for the longest time and then, 'All right, I'll do your damn cover.' And he did it, and nobody cared. It just bombed. And we had great stuff on the inside, but yeah, I lost that one."

In 1989, Dave released a limited-edition bronze Rocketeer statue sculpted by Kent Melton, and in July, *Rocketeer Adventure Magazine* #2 hit the stands. The issue was co-written by *Rocketeer* screenwriters Danny Bilson & Paul De Meo, with page breakdowns by Michael Kaluta, who also contributed another backup story.

Bob Schreck: "Diana was the actual editor on the *Rocketeer* books from Comico. She got two issues out of Dave, within a year of each other, which was pretty, pretty incredible. And that was Diana, our Mussolini, in terms of getting things done. She could make those trains run."

Danny Bilson: "We didn't come from writing comics to film. We went from film to writing comics, with *The Rocketeer* as the first comic we wrote, with no training. When it came to laying out the panels and editing, it's a completely different art form, and you have to do some directing. I know some writers just write scripts and let the artists completely go, but with Dave, it had to be meticulously plotted out. And when we wrote the next two things, we only knew how to write the way we wrote with Dave."

Michael Kaluta: "When Dave was trying to start the second part of *Cliff's New York Adventure*, he said that he was up against the wall, would I do breakdowns, thumbnails? I said, 'Well, I'll try.' And when I started trying, of course, I was trying to draw *Rocketeer* stuff, and, oh, it looked miserable!"

Bruce Timm: "The thing about Dave is, and this sounds weird, I don't think drawing came easy to him, even though he drew from a very early age. He said that, 'Starting with a blank sheet of paper is like the scariest thing. I don't really know what I want to draw.'"

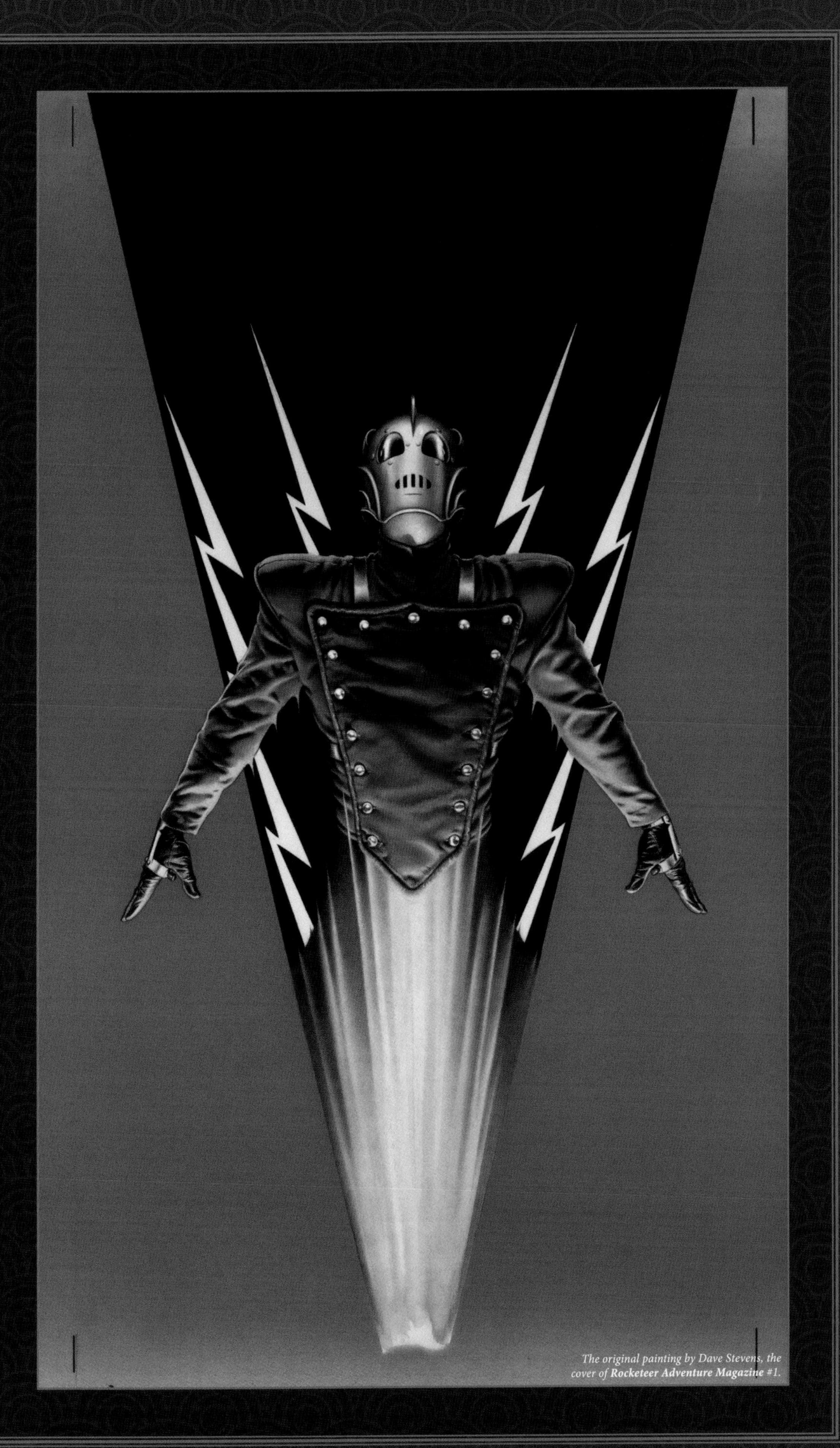

The original painting by Dave Stevens, the cover of ***Rocketeer Adventure Magazine*** *#1.*

Dave on the film set in front of beloved Granville Gee bee plane.

Michael Kaluta: "In *Rocketeer Adventure Magazine* #2, when Cliff gets to Manhattan. It was a huge down shot of Cliff zipping over the top of a bunch of buildings. I had sketched it in, and Dave called me over. 'You got to help me with this.' I said, 'The top of the buildings are black. Then it graduates as it gets down to where your light would be.' As Al Williamson often said, don't draw for color. Draw for the picture. I like handing out Al Williamson advice to anybody, even Dave Stevens."

David Scroggy: "It was really interesting what Kaluta would provide with the thumbnails and how that would grow into pages, what Dave chose to keep and what he chose to eliminate."

Michael Kaluta: "It was actual magic. He transformed my scribbles into Dave Stevens' drawings. The Rocketeer had those rivets, and he just sweated over it all day. All afternoon he was drawing these rivets, and then inking very carefully. Dave had the full pizza pie! There was nothing doubtful about his work."

While Comico had proven to be a quality independent comic publisher, a mid-1986 decision to distribute to the newsstand market proved disastrous. The company significantly raised their print runs for each issue produced, which also increased the percentage of unsold copies being returned. By 1989, Comico was deep into bankruptcy, and the third issue of *Rocketeer Adventure Magazine* was put on hold indefinitely until ownership of Comico's assets was resolved.

Bob Schreck: "And then Comico folded. We hit that wall, and that was it. The finances were gone, so it hurt a lot of folks. It was another one of those things where we thought we knew everything that was happening, but you make some good calls and you make some bad calls. It was combination of no real financial planning, and the newsstand market just killed us."

John Koukoutsakis: "Those early days were kind of like the Wild West for comics. The independents started popping up, and everybody

Dave and Billy Campbell on the **Rocketeer** set.

was like, 'Hey, this is a brilliant idea.' Dave, unfortunately, was in that beginning edge where you're like, okay, this is where it's going to start, but you're not going to get the big bucks. It's those Image guys that are going to get the big bucks later. A lot of those publishers were working on shoestring budgets and suddenly, boom! They're filing for bankruptcy or shutting down, and Dave was getting screwed by publishers in Europe who weren't paying him. If you get lawyers involved, it costs money, and Dave didn't have it."

Bob Schreck: "When Comico went under, all the contracts you have as a company become assets. So, when Andrew Rev purchased Comico, he wound up trying to take everything. It wasn't happy days for Dave."

In 1990, Disney began production on *The Rocketeer* film with Industrial Light & Magic alumnus Joe Johnston as director. Location filming began in August and wrapped in early 1991.

William Stout: "Just an example of the kind of loyalty Dave inspired in his friends: Joe Johnston was the director of *The Rocketeer*, and he and Dave became pretty close. And, one day, Jeffrey Katzenberg called Joe Johnston into his office for a presentation. Joe showed up, and Katzenberg had commissioned all these new designs of the Rocketeer's helmet that were radically different from Dave's design. Katzenberg was very proud of the work that had been done, and he said, 'Well, what do you think?' And Joe Johnston said, 'Oh, I think they're great. Who are you going to get to direct the film?'"

Joe Johnston (Director of *The Rocketeer*): "The helmet is such an iconic image of what the movie is. You can't really change that. We all felt like we were sort of on the Dave Stevens team. We wanted Dave to be happy with the way things looked and make sure that we were presenting his vision as closely as we could."

Danny Bilson: "He got access because we all loved and respected *The Rocketeer* comic book

Dave in the Bulldog diner during production of the film.

and the art of the comic book. So Dave had an intimate experience with the movie that would normally not happen for a comic book artist whose book was licensed."

Marv Wolfman (Comic book writer): "We did some *Rocketeer* stories for *Disney Adventures* while Russ Heath was doing the movie adaptation. *Disney Adventures* was a digest, so the panels were tiny. Dave happened to come into the office that day, just by coincidence, and I was showing it to him. Now, he's in the middle of making a movie. He's one of the producers on the movie, so his time was limited. He looked at it and said, 'I've got to fix the costume.' He took all the art, went to one of the art rooms, sat down, and re-inked half the stuff to make it right. It wasn't even his stuff, but the Rocketeer had to be the Rocketeer."

Russ Heath: "I did *The Rocketeer* comic book that came out with the movie, and it was interesting going over the movie sets and stuff, and Dave was very much involved in the making of the movie. We just stayed friends always, and I would call him up and say, 'What ink are you using right now?' and stuff like that."

The movie premiered on June 19, 1991, at the newly renovated El Capitan Theater in Hollywood, and was officially released June 21. Dave was occupied by promotional activities for the film in the United States and Europe for the rest of the year. He did multiple interviews with Entertainment Tonight, including one shot on location inside the actual Hughes H-4 Hercules aircraft, aka the Spruce Goose, which at the time was on display in nearby Long Beach, California.

Mark Evanier: "He made a real, full, honest-to-God Hollywood movie and had a real, honest-to-God, Hollywood premiere and everything."

Jim Silke: "Dave was reaching for something that he got in the comic. It's there. But getting it in a movie is you trying to do it with a hundred people. It's just damn difficult. You've already got superheroes that fly, and here's a guy who has trouble with a rocket pack. And that's the genius of that, right? It's hard to make the damn thing work. He keeps falling out of the sky! It's a great device because it has its practical, everyday, domestic problems. And that's what makes a good adventure story."

Mark Evanier: "It was a major accomplishment at a time when very few people were independents. And when people at DC and Marvel were saying, 'You should give us your characters because we can get movies made of them and you can't.' Dave got a movie made of his character. And it is now commonplace for creator-owned characters to become motion pictures. It was not when Dave made that happen."

Glen Murakami: "I saw it at the El Capitan. That was exciting because they had refurbished the El Capitan and presented *The Rocketeer* like an

*The premiere of **The Rocketeer** at the El Capitan theater in Los Angeles. Standing with Dave is his occasional model Jewel Shepard.*

old movie with a '40s-style opening live stage show. They had dancers and everything. That was pretty impressive and felt like a big effort."

Joe Johnston: "It was a lot of fun. Looking back on it, I have to say I had the most fun with *The Rocketeer* than I had on anything else, before or since."

After the Rocketeer's Hollywood adventure, Dave turned his attentions to finally finishing the *Cliff's New York Adventure* story. In 1992, after the legal issues with Comico were resolved, Dave moved *The Rocketeer* to Dark Horse Comics.

John Koukoutsakis: "The publisher pool was getting smaller, and I think that Comico going under, Eclipse and Pacific all folding within a short period of time of each other—they demoralized Dave even more. Luckily, he had people he knew at Dark Horse."

Bob Schreck: "The Comico nightmare finally ended after a couple of years. Dave knew Mike Richardson, so after working with Bob Chapman for about eight months, we wound up at Dark Horse."

David Scroggy: "Even though I was vice president of publishing, I wasn't really involved when he came to Dark Horse. I started working

*A panel from **Cliff's New York Adventure**, layouts by Michael Kaluta.*

with Dark Horse in 1994, and Dave was already attached to Bob Schreck at that point for publishing. I got a kind of perverse pleasure out of watching Bob standing in the shoes that I had been in long before, trying to wrangle the pages of *Rocketeer* from Dave Stevens."

Bob Schreck: "He was too much of a perfectionist, and it was harder and harder for him focus and get it together. He was definitely having struggles the further we went on the project."

David Scroggy: "With Pacific Comics—honest to God, we tried everything. We tried threats. We tried cajoling. We tried bribery. We tried throwing ourselves on the floor and begging. We tried everything, and Dave was just immune to it. Bob tried everything I tried and more, and it didn't work any better for Bob than it did for me."

Bob Schreck: "We actually, I guess, had Arthur Adams pencil one issue."

John Koukoutsakis: "I remember that it was a kind of a crazy time. I mean, you're talking about the second volume, *Cliff's New York Adventure.* They had a deadline, and Dave can't meet a deadline."

Bruce Timm: "Dave was always looking to get assistants to help him out on *The Rocketeer*. Except for Jaime, there was really nobody else who'd be up to Dave's standards to help him out, at least on the original one. On the second story, *Cliff's New York Adventure*, he actually had a lot of help."

Geofrey Darrow: "He was trying to finish up *The Rocketeer* and had to draw the interior of an abandoned tenement building, and he wanted know if I could do some backgrounds. And I did a few for him, and I think that was it. He was thinking of redesigning the Rocketeer pack, and he asked me to do a couple passes on it. I mean, we weren't very compatible in that sense, because I'd put all the wrinkles on things, and he'd take them all out."

William Wray: "He increasingly became a perfectionist to the point where work was no fun for him. And that segued into getting other guys to pencil for him, like Kaluta."

Geofrey Darrow: "He needed people who could really draw. Because a lot of guys could draw, but they would draw stylized. I suggested Arthur Adams and Gary Gianni. And Sandy Plunkett, I think. Dave spent some time over there in Paris working with these two guys, Stan Manoukian and Vince Roucher, that he met through French publisher Fershid Bharucha."

John Koukoutsakis: "So, bring in the troops and these guys, Dave pre-approved, these guys. They would help him finish up the book so it can get published, and they did. They came through and got it done."

David Scroggy: "I think you could ask everybody who was attached in the so-called capacity of editor if they were able to insert themselves into

Dave Stevens' art process and ask them how many of them tell you that they did. I think not very many."

For years, Dave had searched for Bettie Page's whereabouts without success. In 1993, she re-emerged via a telephone interview with Robin Leach, a British journalist and host of the television series *Lifestyles of the Rich and Famous*.

Scott Shaw! (Cartoonist)**:** "I think Dave discovered her in some old pinup magazines or something. He was fascinated with everything from that era, and of all the pinup girls, she was probably, even with her clothes on, she was the prettiest of any of them."

Bob Chapman: "When he talked about Betty, it wasn't in a lechy sort of way. It was in a way of respect; he liked her schtick. She did this act of innocence and purity while she was taking off her clothes."

Jim Silke: "There's an ordinariness to Bettie Page that probably attracted Dave. Here was this individually minded young woman who had a great figure and was very proud of her poses. She was great to draw."

Olivia De Berardinis (Pinup artist)**:** "After the sweet pinups of the 1950s, Bettie brought a whole new sexuality to the forefront and then became a cult type of personality during the '70s and '80s."

David Scroggy: "He was relentless until he found her. Had they been of the same generation, he probably would've wound up marrying her."

On March 31, 1994, Dave finally met his lifelong muse, Bettie Page, in person. They became the closest of friends. Dave would remain her advocate and protector for the rest of his life.

Betty, modeled after famed pinup model Bettie Page.

John Koukoutsakis: "Dave called me up and said, 'I found her.' 'What do you mean you found her?' 'I knew she lived in the area. She lives really close!' And he had somehow gotten in contact. He didn't tell me exactly how it happened, but he talked to her, and he had all this royalty money he had set aside for her, for various projects he did. They hit it off right away because she loved his interpretation of her in his comics."

Bob Chapman: "Dave, from the very beginning, was hoping that Bettie would be found because he wanted to share some of the monetary benefits."

William Stout: "Dave was the first person, himself, to pay her for that. And then Dave would hunt down other people who were using her image and force them to pay her as well."

Mark Evanier: "Dave was getting immersed in her life at that point. He would end up

A house ad for ***Rocketeer Adventure Magazine*** *#3.*

driving her to doctor's appointments. He bought her groceries."

John Koukoutsakis: "Dave really, really loved her. Like, not in a sexual way, but if you said that she was his sister or an aunt. He would do anything for her, and at times, she wanted to spend the day hanging out and he didn't have time because he was busy doing something else, but he would make time for her, and he was really sweet to her."

Brinke Stevens: "I thought it was so charming that he was 'driving Miss Bettie,' that he would take her to appointments and just hang out with her and be her companion and her chauffeur."

David Scroggy: "Dave also wanted her to know that the world really did remember her. So he would anonymously take her around to places so she could see just how much she was back in the public eye."

Jennifer Bawcum (Dave's sister)**:** "I have letters where she would tell him that he was the best friend she'd ever had, bar none."

The third and final issue of *Rocketeer Adventure Magazine* was published in January 1995. It did not perform up to expectations sales-wise, and Dave was informed by Dark Horse that the book was too expensive to continue publishing. That was the last new *Rocketeer* story by Dave Stevens.

Bruce Timm: "That last issue of *The Rocketeer* came out pretty much when the comic book market was crashing. He had plans to continue the comic, and even Dark Horse was just, 'Yeah, well, I don't know if we even want to do it, because it's going to take you forever to do, and it's expensive.'"

John Koukoutsakis: "They were cutting those titles that weren't selling well. Dark Horse had to contract, and basically Dave got the cut."

David Scroggy: "I got to see *The Rocketeer* at the beginning of its arc with Pacific Comics and at the end of its arc with Dark Horse. It was just kind of funny to be at the alpha and the omega of that."

Geofrey Darrow: "Between the first and last issue of that last *Rocketeer,* I think he kind of set a record. But his comics were always worth the wait."

In September 1996, Dark Horse Comics released *Cliff's New York Adventure* from *Rocketeer Adventure Magazine* #1–3 collected in a softcover graphic novel. Dave was at a bit of a loss about what to try next with the Rocketeer. He contemplated writing Rocketeer stories for other artists to draw, such as Adam Hughes and Glen Murakami. He would oversee the art and only need to draw covers and do occasional inking. Unfortunately, nothing ever came of it.

Adam Hughes: "Dave was surprised when I said that I would love to do a Rocketeer story. And he said that... I had to be reminded that Bettie was not a giant Russ Meyer maiden. We

Page 1.

SUPERMAN/ROCKETEER 1938

ISSUE ONE.

PAGE ONE/TWO.

We open with a group of petty criminals (the BIX BENTLEY GANG) late at night in a scientific facility in New Jersey [maybe run by that professor who was featured in the Superman television show (Professor Hamiliton?) -- maybe this adventure is where Superman meets him for the first time]. We learn that one of the group (JOEY) has been earning money doing maintenance work in the place, while they plan their next robbery.

? PROF -

Joey has uncovered an invention that the facility has created, which has been tested and is due to be down to the military in the next few days.

We see (although it's shadowy and ill-defined) that the device is a circa 1938 robot. The gang decide to steal the robot and truck it into town where they'll use it to commit their next robbery.

"Tonight?" Joey asks.

"Why not," Bix Bentley replies. "It's mid-week. Quiet. What could go wrong?"

? SUNDAY NITE WAS B'CAST.

PAGE THREE.

We introduce CLIFF SECORD refueling his Cee Bee in Trenton NJ. He thinks about returning home, having learned from a phone call, that Betty awaits him there.

However, he glances over at a nearby airstrip diner and notes people rushing out in panic and confusion. Cars collide as people try to hurriedly drive off. Pilots are running for their planes.

Cliff runs over to investigate.

PAGE FOUR/FIVE

Inside the diner, Welles' War Of The World broadcast has thrown the place into panic. Cliff is equally shocked, believing every word.

Some of the men decide to go off and fight the Martians at their nearby landing sight.

Cliff agrees to go with them and is leaving the diner when he hears a scream. One of the planes that has taken off is in trouble. It's a plane that should have been grounded, but a pilot in panic took it up anyway.

NO!

Cliff runs back to his plane and pulls out the rocket pack and helmet...

At the same time...

A page from the rejected Superman/Rocketeer crossover plot.

Dave and Kent Melton, with a portion of Kent's sculpture for ***The Rocketeer*** *motion picture.*

agreed that if he ever needed, I would do one. He was like, 'I'll hold you to that. Don't say yes if you don't mean it.' And I was like, 'No, I do mean it.' And I would've done it in a heartbeat if he had ever called."

Glen Murakami: "The Rocketeer story he described to me would be Cliff and Betty go to the desert, and there was a giant Tesla coil. I can't remember if they met Tesla, or there was just the Tesla coil. He was going to start several artist teams each working on a chapter. Then I don't know what happened. I don't know why that stalled out."

In 1998, Dave wrote scripts for a three-issue Rocketeer/Superman miniseries that he pitched to DC Comics. But unfortunately, DC rejected the idea.

Jim Silke: "He wanted to do the Rocketeer and Superman. He had the Rocketeer, Superman, and the Orson Welles' broadcast about the Mars invasion. He'd put that all together in a comic book, and I warned him."

Geofrey Darrow: "Kind of a Fleischer Superman."

Jim Silke: "I said, Superman is sacred to the people who own Superman, and if they're going do that, they're probably going to want to own *The Rocketeer*, and then maybe they don't want it enough to buy it. It was a tough thing to put together. Again, it's the business side of it. The idea was great."

Scott Dunbier (Editor)**:** "It was a cool idea—the War of the Worlds broadcast is a perfect MacGuffin for Superman and Rocketeer—but there were some issues in the story that DC objected to. When you do a crossover with a major company, everything has to be very balanced for them, and apparently it wasn't balanced enough."

Laura Martin's coloring for Aurora, which eventually led to Laura coloring ***The Rocketeer****.*

Thomas Jane at the El Capitan Theater in 2011, attending the 20th anniversary screening of ***The Rocketeer*** *film.*

John Koukoutsakis: "After the debacle with DC and Rocketeer/Superman, I think Dave lost a whole lot of interest in this stuff. I think he was just, I don't want to say burned out from *The Rocketeer*, but I think he'd seen a lot of crap that didn't go his way."

Jim Silke: "Dave saw things in the terms of the success at the top of the field rather than somewhere at the bottom. They should have been smart enough to do it. But the leadership at Marvel or DC wasn't that good in those days. It was the '60s fan boys that ran things, and they weren't the people that built the comics. They loved them, but the invention wasn't there."

Jessie Horsting: "*The Rocketeer* was designed as an adventure series, and I know that Dave had in mind many adventures."

In 1999, Randy Bowen produced a resin version of the Kent Melton–sculpted Rocketeer statue, a limited-edition of one thousand. That same year, Dave was diagnosed with hairy cell leukemia, a rare and aggressive form of the disease. He went into remission after chemotherapy treatments but would then be plagued by health issues related to the leukemia and its treatment.

In 2006, Dave began working with editors Arnie and Cathy Fenner on a coffee-table retrospective art book titled *Brush with Passion*. It became his main priority.

Laura Martin (*Rocketeer* colorist): "Two friends of mine, Kelvin Mao and David Mandel, knew Dave Stevens pretty well and asked if I would be interested in digitally coloring a couple of pinups for Dave's *Brush with Passion*. I was surprised because I didn't know that Dave Stevens was even aware that I existed. But I was also honored and happy to be considered and wanted to do the best job I possibly could."

Scott Dunbier: "Laura Martin is really one of the premier colorists in comics, and she has been for a long time. She's won several Eisner Awards—deservedly so."

Kelvin Mao: "Dave Stevens did not follow current comics that closely, and I had to kind of convince him to give a digital colorist a try."

Laura Martin: "Dave emailed me a Catwoman piece with a few notes about her colors and the background. He was very gracious and admitted that he was not familiar with computer coloring and unsure about this whole process."

Kelvin Mao: "Laura, of course, did a fantastic job. Dave was pleasantly surprised by the results and asked if she would color a second piece."

Laura Martin: "The two pieces were very different. The Catwoman was a darker palette, and the Aurora splash page was much brighter, so much more sunny. And I wanted to get the sun on the skin, the brighter, lighter tones and everything that suggested a completely different lighting situation. There were some exchanges, a few little minor changes, but he was very impressed and really happy with the results."

Kelvin Mao: "Dave immediately wanted to give Laura more work, but her schedule just couldn't accommodate it at the time."

Around that time, some of Dave's close friends, including actor Thomas Jane, encouraged him to pursue publishing a *Rocketeer* collection.

Thomas Jane (Actor)**:** "Dave had an ambivalent attitude toward *The Rocketeer*. He felt like the whole thing had been forgotten. I worked at saying, 'Dave, this stuff changed my life, and there's a whole new batch of kids out there. They don't even know this exists. This deserves a new generation's worth of eyeballs. Of hearts and minds, man.' A small group of friends slowly convinced Dave that maybe that might be a good idea. Let it have its rebirth."

But it wasn't until 2007 that Dave started to consider it a serious possibility. At this point,

Dave Stevens' beautifully designed headstone.

David Mandel and Kelvin Mao, longtime friends of Dave Stevens and instrumental in keeping his legacy alive.

***The Rocketeer* had been out of print for over a decade.**

Kelvin Mao: "Sometime later in 2007, Dave and I were discussing, for the umpteenth time, the idea of a complete *Rocketeer* collection. Dave was adamant the art needed to be completely recolored. Much of the early color used different techniques over the 13 to 14 years Dave drew the stories. And he wanted it all to match. This time I asked if he had a colorist in mind, and at first, he wasn't sure. I said, 'Well, how about Laura?' His eyes lit up. 'You really think she would do it? Oh, yeah, I'd definitely want her! If she was interested.' Dave could be almost jarringly humble. 'Of course she'd want to do it,' I thought. The problem was, what publisher would be willing to foot the bill?"

In late 2007, Dave's health took a sudden turn for the worse.

Jennifer Bawcum: "In November of 2007, Dave wound up in the hospital, and that's when they found out that he had congestive heart failure, and that was a result of the chemo. So, November to March is when he declined rapidly."

Dave's failing health prevented him from working very much over the last three or four months of his life. But he did charge David Mandel and Kelvin Mao with pursuing the *Rocketeer* collection under the specifications he'd laid out.

Kelvin Mao: "I was over at Dave's house in early 2008 helping his mother, Carolyn, prepare to move Dave closer to family, where they could take care of him. Dave sat me down and gave his blessing for David Mandel and me to pursue a *Rocketeer* collection. He said he trusted us and to just keep him informed."

Jennifer Bawcum: "We had rented him a house in Turlock, but he was too sick to live there by himself. So, he was living with Mom and he continued to decline."

Dave's sister Jennifer and mother, Carolyn, at the 2010 San Diego Comic-Con.

After a nine-year battle with leukemia, almost a decade of seizing each day as an opportunity to create something and do his best work, Dave Stevens passed away on March 11 in Turlock, California.

Kelvin Mao: "After Dave passed away, David Mandel and I re-doubled our efforts looking for the right opportunity to publish a *Rocketeer* collection. A number of prominent leads didn't work out, but then I think it was David who heard that Scott Dunbier had left DC Comics. Scott was an old friend of ours from art collecting and was a prominent art dealer prior to his career as an editor."

Scott Dunbier: "I left DC Comics in June of 2007 but had a contract that was good until the end of March 2008. When I started at IDW on April 1, 2008, it was sort of a perfect time for me and *The Rocketeer*. I had spoken to Kelvin and David at length about it while on my leave, sabbatical, whatever you want to call it. I gave Ted Adams, the president of IDW at the time, a list of projects I wanted to do, many of which DC wouldn't let me do. *The Rocketeer* was one of the major ones, and Ted was all for it."

Kelvin Mao: "Scott was the ideal person to handle the project, in the right position at the

Dave with his good friend and sometimes collaborator Jim Silke.

right time. And IDW agreed to have Laura recolor the art."

Laura Martin: "I was incredibly surprised, elated, and honored that Dave wanted me to color it. There was no way I could say no. I absolutely was on board the minute I was asked."

Scott Dunbier: "It's a big deal because we were able to get the person Dave wanted, and that was always the most important thing to me."

Laura Martin: "It was not easy to figure my way through the project. It had been colored by so many people at different times. I don't want to be that person who just takes the job and says, 'I can do it better.' All I wanted to do was to capture Dave's vision."

On December 16, 2009, *The Rocketeer: The Complete Adventures* and *The Rocketeer: The Complete Adventures Deluxe Edition* were released. Thomas Jane wrote a heartfelt introduction for the deluxe edition.

Jennifer Bawcum: "IDW just did a phenomenal job, collecting all the chapters of *The Rocketeer* into one volume."

Thomas Jane: "That omnibus was our homage. That was our gift to Dave. So I have a personal relationship to it that will always be there and really kind of a gift to us as a way of holding on to and honoring what we loved about Stevens and his work."

Scott Dunbier: "It was a big success. The books sold very well, probably better than we even thought, and they were a critical success."

Jackie Estrada: "The Eisner Awards are referred to as the Oscars of the comics industry. And at the 2010 Eisner Awards, I knew that *The*

Dave Stevens, A.K.A. Cliff Secord, A.K.A. The Rocketeer.

Rocketeer collection was going to be winning. I contacted Thomas Jane about being a presenter."

Jennifer Bawcum: "The award was Best Archival Collection in a project for comic books. Mom went up and accepted the award from Tom Jane. It was just a really sweet evening, just celebrating Dave and his legacy."

Scott Dunbier: "It was a big effort by many people, and I take great pride in the achievement that we all made."

In 2010, *Dave Stevens' The Rocketeer Artist's Edition* was released, the very first book of its kind.

Scott Dunbier: "An Artist's Edition is basically taking original art, scanning it at high resolution in color, so while it appears to be in black and white, it's actually in color. You can see blue pencil notations, white-out, gradients in the ink. It basically shows you all the bits and pieces, the little nuances that make original art unique."

In 2011, *The Rocketeer Artist's Edition* won two Eisner Awards at Comic-Con International for Best Archival Collection/Project–Comic Books, and Best Publication Design. As of this writing, over 120 Artist's Edition–style books (more than 80 from IDW alone) have been published. 2022, the 40th anniversary of the first *Rocketeer* story by Dave Stevens, saw a new miniseries released by Stephen Mooney, *The Rocketeer: The Great Race*, as well as new editions of *Dave Stevens' The Rocketeer Artist's Edition* and *The Rocketeer: The Complete Adventures Deluxe Edition*.

Dave Stevens.

Unused cover by Stephen Mooney.

Dave Stevens'

THE ROCKETEER®